REVOLUTION

THE TASTE OF FREEDOM

Book One of the *America's Beginning's Trilogy*

DAVID P. MCINTYRE

Published 2025

Printed in the United States of America

First Edition

ISBN (softcover): 978-1-967842-81-0
ISBN (e-book): 978-1-967482-82-7

For information, address:

Holzer Books LLC
8 The Green, Ste. A
Dover, Delaware 19901 USA

For information about special discounts available for bulk purchases, sales promotions, and educational needs, contact:

info@holzerbooksllc.com
+1 (888) 901-7776

holzerbooksLLC©

Preface

"Revolution, The Taste of Freedom" is a story of two families, The Rutledge's and the Reed's, living during the time of the Revolutionary War in America. They came to America prior to the war seeking a new life. They settled just outside of Boston, Massachusetts.

Boston was in one of thirteen British colonies in the new world. There was Massachusetts, Vermont, New Hampshire, Rhode Island, New York, New Jersey, Delaware, Maryland, Pennsylvania, Virginia, North Carolina, South Carolina and Georgia. Maine was not officially a separate colony at that time.

The two couples arrived in America a few years after a Great Awakening that began in England and brought to America. It was a Christian revival and reinforced their faith and commitment to Christ and to teach the Bible to their future children. They also found themselves in the colonies during the French and Indian War. That war was between France and England; some Indians fought on both sides. The war ended in 1763 with the British winning. Wars are costly. The King of England, King George III, sought to recoup the cost by taxing the colonies. Those living in the colonies thought of themselves as Englishmen and that they were being unfairly treated.

They had helped in the war effort; even supplying money for the effort. They did not think it was right that they were now being treated as though they were a conquered people, slaves to England. The colonial atmosphere began to simmer against England like a pot being heated. As new sanctions were imposed it went to boiling resentment, and finally to a boil over that led to a Declaration of Independence and the Revolutionary War against England.

The story begins with the birth of the Rutledge and Reed children before the war, sees the events through their eyes leading up to the war, and then follows Joshua and Caleb, the two oldest sons of the two families, as they engage in the war.

Prologue

To understand the story of "The Taste of Freedom," we must go back in time to see what led up to the events. No! We will not go all the way back to God's creation of everything, but we will say the story is about God and His interaction with man. Since the very beginning, Satan has always fought against God and tried to drive a wedge between God and man. It has been a continuous war. By 1500 AD, the outlook in England and Europe was dismal, somber, depressing, and gloomy. The common folks were practically slaves under feudal Lords bent on power and wealth. It wasn't much better under the priesthood of the Church. The Church had sole access to God's Word and were the sole interpreters of it. If you wanted good "interpretations" you paid for them. Wars had devastated the land. Those of faith even thought that the end times were near. Satan was proud of his work. The only bright spot was the discovery by some more adventurous soles of a new world across the Atlantic Ocean to the west.

God, though, was still working. In 1517, a German monk by the name of Martin Luther studied the Bible and discovered many discrepancies between what God's Word said and the teachings of the Church. He published his findings and basically started the Protestant Reformation. The leaders of the movement tried at first to reform the Church, but the Church resisted. Protestant denominations were formed, Lutheran, Baptist, and others. There were others that challenged the Church in England.

Even Kings challenged the Church, mostly though, for their own selfish ends. King Henry VIII in England, for example, in 1534 wanted the Pope to annul his marriage to Catherine of Aragon so he could marry someone else. When the Pope refused, he broke with the Church eventually leading to the establishment of a rival Church of England. He and other kings felt they could now control that church. Some kings did good. King James commissioned the translation of the Bible from the original languages into English. It was published in 1611 and was known as "The King James Bible." It brought the Word of God to the common man.

So, what do these events have to do with our story? Everything! This new Bible allowed the common man to study the Bible for themselves. They, like Luther and others, discovered for themselves that the established church teachings were at odds with what God's Word said. At first in England, they tried to reform and purify the church. They became known as the "Puritans". When they were unsuccessful, a group of them decided to leave England and go to this new world across the sea. They were called Separatists (Pilgrims). One hundred and two of them under the leadership of William Bradford left England along with thirty crewmen aboard the Mayflower and sailed across the Atlantic to this new world. It took sixty-six days to make the crossing. It was an ordeal; even worse when they arrived. They had to endure a brutal winter that took nearly half their lives. The others may not have survived, except for God's providence. A Native American Indian named Squanto who had been captured, made a slave, and brought to England. There he was taught English, later freed and brought back to the new world. During his time in England, he became a Christian. He arrived just in time to save the Puritans. Why did they endure all of this? The answer is freedom; the freedom to worship as they chose without interference.

Between 1730 and 1740 there was a great revival which later became known as the First Great Awakening, led by such men as George Whitfield and Jonathon Edwards. The emphasis was on personal commitment to Christ versus tradition, ritual and the personal study of God's Word. That also did not find favor with the King nor the Church of England. Those folks also wanted to worship as they chose and began emigrating to the new world.

There were many others that made the trip across for the same reason and from other countries. Some, like the Puritans, came for religious freedom. Others came to be free from the heavy hand of the feudal landlords in England and Europe. They came to escape the tyranny of Kings, feudal lords and the Church to come to America to worship as they chose and to live and work to build a better life for themselves. They wanted a taste of freedom.

Our story now begins with two couples who made the trip across the Atlantic in the mid 1700's. By that time, immigration from England and Europe had swelled the population of the new world to over two million people. French colonists settled primarily in what later became known as Canada. The Spanish settled primarily to the south in what would later become Florida, Texas, Mexico, and South America. The English established colonies along the eastern seaboard from Maine to Georgia. The English colonies were initially helped and supported by the English King and given a certain autonomy. They thrived. Then England went to war against France. The war came to the colonies; battles were fought on the lands of the new world. The English colonies helped by sending supplies and men to fight to defeat the French. The conflict was known as the French and Indian War and occurred between 1754 and 1763, ending with a British Victory. It left the British Crown heavy in debt. Those thriving colonies in the new world, which had just been a curiosity, would soon become the means to recoup the war losses. The colonists were about to discover that the tyranny they had escaped from was about to travel across the ocean to them.

Characters

Thomas and Elizabeth Rutledge

    Joshua – born 1758
    Sarah – born 1759, died in 1760
    Mark – born 1761
    Hannah – born 1762
    Paul – born 1764 Reed Family

John and Mary Reed

    Caleb – born 1758
    Sarah – born 1761
    Charles – born 1762
    William – born 1763
    Jonathon – born 1765
    Maria – born 1766

Pitman's

    Father John Pitman
    Jessica – born 1758
    Uncle and Aunt Martha

Contents

I would like to thank the members of my family that helped me in the writing of this book. I would like to thank first my patient wife who tried her best to encourage and give me insight in some of the passages, i want to thank my brother, Dennis A. McIntyre, who has also published several books for his careful reading and corrections of the manuscript. I also wish to thank my niece, Tricia Gallager, for some good insight and suggestions. Thank you all.

David P. McIntyre

Chapter 1
Simmering

Thomas Rutledge and his wife, Elizabeth, were two of the many that endured the long ocean voyage and came across to the new world around 1850. They had barely enough money to secure passage on the ship. Land speculators in England, who had been given large grants of land from the King of England, advertised for workers who would be willing to become indentured servants on plantations in the new world. The contract called for five years' service in exchange for fifty acres. Thomas and Elizabeth decided to sign the contract. The work on the plantation was hard. They postponed starting a family until the contract was fulfilled. As promised, they were given fifty acres just outside of Boston in the Massachusetts colony. The first two years on their own land were difficult. Thomas had to build a house, clear and work the land. Elizabeth worked right alongside him. They knew the Bible commandment to work only six days and rest on the seventh. So, they obeyed. That day was set aside for church and rest. They attended a small church nearby pastored by Josiah Bartlet. There they met other couples like themselves, including John and Mary Reed.

The Reeds came across to Boston but not as indentured servants. They found work on the docks in Boston harbor. They scrimped and saved for several years. Then they were able to buy a fifty-acre parcel of land about a mile from the Rutledge's. The Rutledge's and the Reed's became close friends and helped each other sharing tools and equipment. It was common for them to share meals together, particularly on Sundays.

It wasn't long before both couples wanted to start a family. Elizabeth and Mary became pregnant and when the time came close, they talked to each other about what names to call their children. The week before Elizabeth gave birth, Pastor Josiah had been preaching about the two spies that had given a good report to Moses about the promise land in Canaan. They knew the story. Only those two spies would finally make it into the promised land. The ten that gave bad reports would die as Israel wandered in the wilderness. They decided that if the babies were boys, they would name them Joshua and Caleb after those Biblical spies. Elizabeth gave birth first on June 4th, 1758, and named her son Joshua. Mary followed, about three weeks later on June 26th and named her son, Caleb.

Joshua was the firstborn of five children, three boys and two girls, born to Thomas and Elizabeth. Sarah was born about a year and a half after Joshua. Then Mark was born fifteen months later followed by Hannah the following year and finally Paul in 1764. Elizabeth had her hands full caring for the young children. Thomas spent most of his time working on the farm to provide for his young family.

It was a similar story with the Reed family. After Caleb came Sarah three years later, followed by Charles the following year, then William in 1765, John in 1767 and Mary in 1769. Each child in colonial families was considered a gift from God. Colonial families were often large, especially on farms. More hands meant more help with the work that needed to be done.

The Rutledge's suffered the loss of their daughter Sarah in her first year. The family grieved but accepted the loss. Colonial life was hard, and most families expected to lose one or more of their children. History had taught them that the Pilgrims on the Mayflower had lost almost half their numbers in that first bitter cold winter they were in the new world. When the Reeds' first daughter was born a year after Sarah Rutledge died, the Reeds named her Sarah in remembrance of Sarah Rutledge. It was a nice gesture that may have helped soothe Rutledge's grief. The bond between the two families was strong and their children grew up together.

Concerning education, all children were expected to attend school at least up to eighth grade. High school was meant for those students who showed more promise. The Great Awakening of the 1730s brought, among other things like the conviction that children are the heritage of the Lord and must be taught God's principles in the Bible. George Whitfield taught that the path to God was through faith in Jesus Christ, not in some church traditions, and required a personal commitment to the Lord. He also taught that parents had a responsibility to teach God's Word to their children. That meant they needed to be taught how to read so they could read the Bible for themselves. That often even carried over to slaves under the care of their masters. Massachusetts in 1647, even passed a "Ye Old Deluder Satan Act" that required towns with fifty or more families to hire teachers to teach children reading and writing. Joshua and Caleb along with their siblings all attended school.

The children also learned about their history. Most families originated as immigrants from England and Europe, seeking religious freedom, or a better way of life. They learned about the Puritan dissenters of the Anglican Church of England seeking religious freedom to study the Bible for themselves instead of being told what to believe by the church clergy. There were even some from Germany and Europe, influenced by Luther's Protestant Reformation, seeking the same freedom. Others just wanted a chance to build something instead of constantly being under the feudal landlords. The colonies seemed like a breath of fresh air to the downtrodden, so they came even though life would be hard. They learned about the Pilgrims and Squanto's compassion for the plight of the new arrivals at Plymouth. They learned how he taught them how to survive in this new land; how to hunt and plant corn for food. The children were able to learn of such stories because of the printing press that had been invented many years before in Germany (1440). The colonists took full advantage of this invention. It provided textbooks for the children including the Bible. It also provided a means for the colonists to communicate among themselves and find out the latest news within the colonies or from abroad.

For Joshua and Caleb, the stories provided fertile fodder for their imaginations. Being from England, they imagined that they were fighting the French in the French and Indian War. Afterall, it was only a few years earlier that the war had ended with an English victory. The war was misnamed because it wasn't really a war against French and all the Indians; some Indians fought with the British. Joshua, Caleb and their siblings could still imagine battle scenes, where they were victorious against the enemy. It was fun. They were kids exercising their imaginations. They took up arms with wooden muskets to fight for liberty, although they may not have known what liberty meant. They would learn.

Sunday meant going to church. Everyone went. They would hear a message from Pastor Josiah from the Bible and sing some favorite hymns like Issac Watts "Alas and Did My Savior Bleed", Martin Luther's "A Mighty Fortress is Our God" or St. Francis Of Assisi's "All Creatures of Our God and King". It was a way of life. Even the slaves were permitted to gather for worship on Sunday. Joshua and Caleb liked to steal away sometimes and go listen outside a black church. Those folks really knew how to worship!

Typically, after church on Sundays, the Reeds' and the Rutledge's would fellowship together at one of their homes. This Sunday, it was the Rutledge house. Their house was a modest farmhouse. A porch extended the entire width of the house and faced west. There were chairs and one rocking chair on it. It was the Rutledge favorite place to gather in the evening to watch a sunset when the weather was good. The main entrance opened to a larger room with a large fireplace to the left with all the tools necessary for the fire were kept. Big iron skillets were hung on the left side for cooking and baking and a large stew pot on the right. Surrounding the fireplace were several chairs and a sofa. A large table was behind the sofa and toward the other end of the room which served for meals, sewing, doing homework and so forth.

Elizabeth stored all her dishes as well as other things in a large buffet next to the table against the front wall of the house. The main bedroom was on the left side in the back of the house facing east. Thomas always wanted to wake up with the sun. A loft extended across the back of the house over the bedroom. Next to the bedroom in the back of the house was a small back room with a bathtub. A door opened out the back of that room leading to an outhouse. Thomas later added a second bedroom on the south side with a loft when the children got older.

Joshua had just come in from the back-room and overheard his parents in a heated discussion regarding the unfairness of the tax acts from the King of England.

"Old King George did it again," shouted Thomas, "he has banned the colonists from settling beyond the Appalachian Mountains"

"Where did you hear that?" questioned Elizabeth.

Thomas clearly agitated by the news, slammed down the circular on the table, "It is right here in big bold letters."

Trying to calm her husband, Elizabeth responded, "Well, I doubt it will affect us."

Still irritated Thomas retorted, "That's not the point. How can George think he has the right to restrict where we settle? He did not come over here and settle this land; we did. We should have the rights to this land. We cleared it worked it, planted it, and developed it. The English aristocracy did nothing!"

Thomas's voice grew louder the more he talked. Joshua was listening and tried not to breathe too hard to alert his parents that he was overhearing the conversation. All the while, he empathized with his father's frustration.

Seeing her husband's anger aroused, Elizabeth continued to try and calm him, "Dear, calm down. It is no use getting excited about it. It probably won't affect us. We have many other things to think about like caring for our family."

Elizabeth's gentle voice always seemed to be able to calm Thomas down when he became irritated. He felt his heart rate decrease and the blood flow away from his hot head as he spoke. "Yeah, I suppose, but if this keeps up, the colonists will become angry. When that anger reaches a boiling point, look out!"

Joshua waited a bit and then after his father had calmed down, came into the room.

"What were you and mom talking about?" asked Joshua.

"Oh, we were just hearing about some new impositions by King George." Elizabeth answered.

"Yeah, He is restricting us from being able to settle in the new lands acquired from the French." Thomas forced himself to speak calmly. "It doesn't really affect us."

About that time, John and Mary Reed arrived and joined The Rutledge's in the house.

John overhearing the end of the conversation about new restrictions by King George, "You must be reading the new circular."

"Yes, come on in and join us." Answered Thomas.

"Yes, please do and welcome, we could use a little distraction," Elizabeth responded while offering hugs to her new guests.

"Is the King doing anything else that might affect us?" asked Joshua.

Thomas, upon reading further down in the circular, his anger visibly apparent, "This Sugar Act might be a problem for us."

"How so?" Elizabeth responded knowing that Thomas would be calmer is he was forced to think through an answer to her question.

"We get cheaper sugar through the smugglers, who bring it in I think from the Caribbean. If we cannot import goods from wherever we desire, the cost of necessities is going to go way up. I do not believe England should have as much control over merchants as they do." Thomas answered more calmly.

"I agree with Tom," John interjected, "trying smugglers in the Admiralty Courts is even worse. That is a flagrant violation of our rights as English citizens."

Glad to have some support in his feelings, Thomas shouted, "You are right! If a smuggler is caught, then he will have to be transported to England for trial and will have to face an English judge.

Mary, who could no longer keep quiet joined in:

"If we are English, how is that a problem?"

Answering his wife calmly, John replied, "The people in England have no idea of the conditions here and what we face nor does the judge. Even if you accept that the smuggling was wrong, which I question, shouldn't that person be tried here and face a jury of his peers?"

"Not only that," chimed in Thomas, "but he also now must leave his family and take a long voyage that could take two months or more each way before the issue is resolved. Meanwhile his family suffers.' How is that fair?

Elizabeth let out a sigh, "I am glad we are not in the smuggling business!"

"Maybe not," Thomas answered emphatically, "but if they get away with that now, what will happen in the future if some law is passed that affect farmers like us and we are then arrested and have to go to England for trial?"

His sternness surprised and frightened her a little, "Wow, I had not thought of that."

Mary added, "Me neither."

The following week both families met at the Reed house. Their house was a little larger but like the Rutledge house. The main room was almost a mirror image of the Rutledge home with the fireplace on the right and the main table on the left. Their bedrooms also faced east. John also as a farmer, liked to have the sun wake him in the morning.

There was another circular announcing that King George III had enacted the Stamp Act placing a tax on paper goods and legal documents.

"Elizabeth, did you see the news that the King has now taxed everything of paper?" Thomas announced angrily.

Elizabeth replied a bit irritated herself, "No Honey, I have been too busy taking care of the house and the kids. What does that mean?"

Thomas responding to his wife's tone tried calm down, "We will now have to pay tax on every newspaper, every legal document, even just plain paper for the kids to write on at school." He was not successful. "They are taxing us to death! I will bet that will not set well with the Sons of Liberty!"

"Who are these Sons of Liberty?"

Thomas finally got the message that Elizabeth was upset with him and answered more calmly, "They are a rebel group; I think led by a man named, Samuel Adams, that is resisting and protesting these new acts by the English monarchy. It would not surprise me if things got more heated than just voicing disapproval of the Acts."

Thomas was right. In Boston, a stamp distributor was hanged in effigy and his shop destroyed. In New York, a howling mob forced a ship master to retreat to a British warship fearing his own safety. The Virginian government openly challenged the Stamp Act. That did not stop the British; they passed another one, the Quartering Act requiring all the colonies to provide housing and food for British troops. Thomas and John were livid. After church one Sunday, John pulled Thomas aside.

"Did you read the news about the Quartering Act?"

"Yeah, that one is hitting too close to home!" answered Thomas. "I have enough trouble supporting my family without having to feed and house brutish British troops as well! Besides, why does the king think he has to maintain a standing army in a time of peace? The French and Indian War has been over for two years now."

John his anger aroused, "I agree! There are about two thousand troops in Boston alone and there are only about sixteen thousand residents. That means all of them may have to house one or more soldiers. My house is small. There is barely enough room for me, my wife and the kids"

"I have the same problem," Thomas responded. "What in the world is King George trying to do; forcing us into declaring independence?"

John brightened, "Now there is a thought..."

Parliament did repeal the Stamp Act as pressure mounted but still maintained they had the right to rule the colonies. The Continental Congress met late in 1766 in Philadelphia to discuss the crisis. Meanwhile The Sons of Liberty celebrated the repeal of the Stamp Act by erecting a Liberty Pole in New York. A liberty pole had been an old tradition of protest dating back to the Roman Empire. It was a flagpole with either a flag or slogans on it. The pole angered the British and they promptly chopped it down. Another one was erected, which was also chopped down. A third pole was erected and stayed up into 1767. The British responded by passing out handbills attacking the Sons of Liberty as enemies of society. The poles did not hurt anyone or destroyed any property; they were just visual symbols of the growing dissent among the colonists against the British. They felt they had the right as British citizens to voice their disagreement. The British were not listening; they passed the New York Restraining Act to prevent the colonists from passing new laws until they complied with the Quartering Act. Thomas and John had to go out in the fields and work off their anger.

Chapter 2

Boiling

Things got worse in the years following. In 1768 Parliament passed a series of acts collectively called the Townsend Acts. Each one was designed to squash the growing spirit of rebellion.

Revenue Act – placed import duties on items such as glass, lead, paint, paper.

Indemnity Act – lowered taxes that the British East India company paid on products like tea resulting in unfair competition with competitors.

Commissioners of Customs Act – designed to improve collection of taxes and reduce smuggling. They wanted to rein in the unruly colonial government. Of course, this was not well received because many of the colonial leaders were smugglers. They did not view themselves as criminals, just merchants seeking less costly goods to sell. They did not feel that the British government thousands of miles away should have that much power over mercantile trade.

Vice-Admiralty Court Act – tighten the rules so that smugglers would be tried in royal naval courts not colonial ones and by judges who could collect five percent of the fines without a jury.

They miscalculated the spirit of the Americans. The Massachusetts Assembly passed a circular letter denouncing all the acts. Originally, most of the Bostonians thought of themselves as English Americans. The same was true of other groups; the Irish thought of themselves as Irish Americans, the Germans as German Americans and so forth. These new acts began to change things. A new group appeared and thought of themselves as just Americans. Joshua and Caleb began hearing discussions like:

"The British have done it again with the new Townsend Acts," Thomas shouted. "I am beginning to think that England no longer considers us as British citizens. Maybe we should no longer think that way too."

"What do you think we ought to do?" Elizabeth asked growing more concerned over her husband's increasing irritability with the British,

"I think we should no longer buy British goods like tea or clothing, Thomas emphatically insisted. "Any group that tries to force us into a certain way of thinking deserves to be punished. One way we can do it is to boycott their products. That way we can hurt them in the only way they will get the message."

"I guess we can do that," Elizabeth responded attempting to curb his anger. "I love English tea, but I can make do with tea from other places. We can also make our own clothes from cloth produced here instead of buying cloth or clothes from England. I will go to the other ladies. I think they will agree."

The tension increased. What was simmering resentment began to reach a boiling point. In January 1770 in Golden Hill, New York, The Sons of

Liberty clashed with British soldiers. The soldiers were trying to pass out pro-British propaganda and several were captured by the colonists. Other soldiers tried to rescue the captured soldiers. Townspeople then surrounded them. An officer ordered the drawing of bayonets to cut through the crowd. Some soldiers and townsfolk were wounded. A group of officers arrived to disperse the soldiers before the whole thing got totally out of hand.

In Boston it was worse. Two thousand soldiers tried to enforce the British laws on the Sixteen thousand inhabitants. Animosity grew among the townspeople, many of whom had been long-term friends. There were some who were very loyal to the king of England and thought of themselves as English citizens. While they did not like the harsh treatment from the soldiers and representatives of the king, they still felt that a proper response was to petition the king for redress of grievances. These were the Loyalists. Others felt they needed to demand that the king cease and desist and if he did not, then they were justified in fighting back. These people thought of themselves as Patriots. There had been clashes between patriots and soldiers, almost from the beginning. Now there were also clashes among former friends who were loyal to the British crown and the patriots who no longer were. The patriots vandalized some of the loyalists' stores, selling British goods, while intimidated merchants and customers. One loyalist defended his store by firing a gun through a window. The shot killed an eleven-year-old boy. Later a street brawl occurred ending with the soldiers killing five colonists. Fortunately, the Rutledge and the Reed families were not present. Their farms occupied much of their time and there was little time left for a trip into the city of Boston. They only made the trip on special occasions. They did see some of the handbills that were being passed out by the soldiers.

"I think I have a use for the British handbills," Thomas told Joshua in anger. "You and Caleb can collect all you want, and I will put them in the outhouse. If Britain is going to crap on the colonies, I guess we can return the favor..." Everyone laughed.

Farm life was a lot of work and required everyone in the family to do their share. The Rutledge home was modest even by colonial standards. It was built of wood, most of it obtained from their land, with wood shingles. Thatched roofs had been discouraged by that time because it was an increased fire hazard. Originally the house had a dirt floor. Later, when things improved, Thomas was able to add a wood floor. There was a fireplace at one end where Elizabeth did most of the cooking. It also heated the house, especially on those cold winter nights. The children generally slept on mats near the fireplace. When the family grew larger, some slept in the loft. Furniture was limited to a table, some chairs, a dresser, a chest, and places to hang things on the walls. A large bowl and a large pitcher of water served as a wash station. Everyone could wash their hands and face before supper or going to bed. Baths were generally once a week events usually on Saturday. They wanted to look clean before going to church on Sunday. There was a room on the back of the house with a wash tub in it. Water was carried in. If it was too cold, some water heated at the fireplace was added. It never really got that warm, but at least it was tolerable. The younger children generally shared the same bath water with the older ones taking their baths first. There was some attempt to ensure modesty and separate the boys from the girls. An outside outhouse served to handle other bodily requirements. Elizabeth did her best to keep the clothes clean, washing them by hand and hanging them on a clothesline to dry. She worked especially hard on Saturday to ensure clean clothes for Sunday.

Thomas was usually up before sunup. By this time, they had a couple of cows which needed milking at 5:30 AM and again at 5:30 PM. The cows provided milk for the family. As the milk settled in the milk pail, cream could be skimmed off the top which Elizabeth, sometimes with the help of the children, turned into butter or cheese. The animals had to be fed, stalls cleaned out, and then the hard work began. It was different depending on the season. In early spring, the fields had to be cleared and plowed. When Thomas and Elizabeth first obtained the farm, there were a lot of trees that had to be cleared out so that the land could be planted. It was back breaking work swinging the axe to topple the trees and even harder to get rid of the stumps.

Over time, Thomas acquired a horse to help, then an ox which was better, and more recently a second ox. Thomas was amazed at how much more work could be done with two oxen. It wasn't just double. It was way more than that. There was one time when one of the oxen became ill and did not pull as hard as the other one. On those days, the amount of work accomplished was drastically reduced. That Sunday, Pastor Josiah preached on "Do not be unequally yoked together with unbelievers".[1] It was as though God had specifically planned for the one ox to be sick that week to give Thomas a clear object lesson in preparation for the pastor's message. Thomas felt God did that a lot. The message hit home. We are not to be "yoked" together with those who pull against us. It also dawned on him that those who do not work are a drag on those that do. The Bible admonition is that if a man will not work, he should not eat. The ox recovered the following week and began to pull strongly again. That was a blessing and reminded Thomas that he was also "not to muzzle the ox that treadeth out the corn."[2]

Thomas taught his children that everyone had to work. There cannot be

---

1. II Corinthians 6:14

2. I Corinthians 9:9

any slackers. In the spring, rocks needed to be removed and placed in the fence rows, the fields plowed and then seeded. Weeds needed to be dealt with as the plants grew so that they did not crowd out the good crops. Everyone needed to be in the fields at harvest time. There was corn and perhaps other grains. There was hay to be cut, dried and brought into the barn. It especially had to be dry, which meant that Thomas had to carefully watch the weather as best he could to ensure the hay would dry before being placed in the barn. Farmers learned the hard way that wet hay in a barn will generate heat that could set the hay on fire and burn the barn down. Hay was needed to feed the animals during winter when the grass was covered with snow.

There were other chores to be done as well. Chickens had to be fed, and eggs collected. Animals had to be watered. There were always repairs. In addition, Thomas planted tobacco in one field. He did not use it himself. In the colonies, tobacco was a cash crop, and the dried leaves could be traded in town for needed supplies. There was very little money in the colonies. The colonial governments did not print or produce coins. The paper and coins came mainly from the British and a lot of that went to the town merchants.

Tobacco was sold to England. Merchants would collect more of the leaves from the farmers by giving them a credit in English pounds, shillings, etcetera. depending on the quantity of leaves brought in. Thomas grew tobacco so he could buy needed supplies in town. That meant that he and his family would have to carefully harvest the leaves, hang them in the barn to dry, and make them ready to trade. It was the same with Caleb's family.

Joshua and Caleb were almost twelve when the Boston Massacre, as it was called, occurred. The farm life had made them into strong strapping boys that already showed signs of manhood. They had heard about the massacre and wanted to go into Boston and see where all occurred. They finished all their chores one day and persuaded their parents to let them go into town. It was still winter and so the yearly field preparation had not yet begun. It took about an hour and a half to get there. There were posters around near the site decrying the outrageous action of the soldiers. They passed by a three-story Tavern with several townsfolk coming and going. Some of the townspeople were willing to talk to them and it soon became apparent that there was a great deal of controversy over the whole affair. Some blamed it on the resistance of the Sons of Liberty.

Some said, "They should not have defied the Parliament Acts as they did, after all we are Englishmen under English rule, and it is not right that we defy the laws."

Others said, "It is not right that the soldiers kill unarmed colonists or that the merchant kill an innocent child. They ought to be tried and hung for that!"

It became obvious to the boys (or better maybe young men) that the clashes and rhetoric between the Loyalists and the Patriots was getting stronger. Fast friends, even family members were now at odds with each other. The animosity was so strong that Joshua and Caleb did not want to agree with either side fearing they would incur the anger of the other side. They decided to back away and headed toward the harbor. Caleb especially wanted to see the tall ships. He was fascinated with the tall ships and the sea. Joshua followed him.

The streets were narrow, unpaved and twisted between several buildings. Eventually they found themselves at the harbor on the south side. It was filled with ships. Most were at anchor, but some were tied securely to a long pier. That pier was impressive. Man-made, and jutted out almost half a mile into the harbor. It provided a place where ships could load and unload their cargo. They had timed it just right to watch in fascination as long boats with long lines to a British warship were maneuvering into a place on the pier.

Boston Harbor

Ships could rarely be sailed to the pier and then only smaller ones. It would take considerable skill from the sailing crew and the right wind conditions to accomplish docking. It might even require turning the ship a hundred and eighty degrees under sail, using the wind as a braking force to bring the ship safely in. Most commanders did not want to try it. Instead, they would lower the sails, anchor the ship as close as they dared to the pier, and await their turn to dock. Strong ropes from the ship would be carried to the pier by small boats. The ship would then be pulled in using winches. The idea was to move the ship in, but not too fast. An onshore wind could be a problem if the ship moved too quickly toward the pier.

Boats on the opposite side at the bow and stern might be used in tandem with the winches, acting as a drag to slow the movement. If they wanted to spin the ship around before approaching the pier, the bow and stern boats, rowing in opposite directions could potentially spin the larger ship on its axis. When the ship was ready to leave the pier, small boats were used to pull the ship sufficiently away from the pier so that the sails could be hoisted, allowing the ship to move out under its own power. It would be especially difficult if the wind was up. Multiple ropes would then be added to properly secure her. The port sailors were very skilled with a lot of experience moving ships in and out. Joshua and Caleb watched in utter fascination.

The ship was a beauty. The boys decided to have a closer look at her. At first, they were rebuffed by a couple of very gruff-looking sailors. When the sailors realized the boys were just curious and were admiring the ship, they softened and began talking about her.

Sailor 1, "She's a fine one, isn't she."

Both boys almost in unison: "she sure is!"

Joshua asked, "How long is she?"

Sailor 2: "She's a hundred-eighty-five feet long" and then added without being asked: "and she is fifty-one feet wide. Her height is over two-hundred feet from her keel to the top of her mast."

"How fast can she go?" asked Caleb.

Sailor 1, "With over six thousand square yards of sail, she can do six to seven knots with a strong wind."

Caleb, "Wow! How many cannons are there? I counted forty on just one side."

Sailor 2, "We have a complement of ninety-eight, and they range from smaller twelve pounders to the big thirty-two ponders on the lowest deck. She will hold her own in a good fight. Just one ship like this one might have more firepower than an entire fort on shore. That is why Great Britain is known for ruling the seas."

Joshua noticing different ships in the harbor, "I see that some ships have more rectangular sails and some more triangular. What is the difference?"

Sailor 1 added, "The ones like this warship, are called frigates. They can potentially handle higher winds and seas. They get pushed from the stern by the wind and the sails are especially made to catch as much of that power to push the ship along. It takes a lot of men to work her. Several sailors go aloft on the masts to lower the sails or pull them back up as needed. The other ships you see like that one over there (he pointed to a ship in the harbor) are called schooners. The sails are raised or lowered with ropes from the deck and the booms can be turned to better catch the wind. Those ships are more maneuverable and often turn more quickly. In some cases, they may even be faster. The warship you see here also has a deeper draft and must stay in deeper water. The deep draft also makes them more stable out at sea. Some of the schooners may have shallower draft and can go in shallower water."

British Warship

Schooner

Joshua and Caleb continued their questions for a while and the sailors were glad to answer them. They were proud of their ship. They couldn't let the boys on board as that was against regulations. The boys learned that there were square plates covering the cannons. Many of the sailors slept between the cannons and often had meals there. The sailors told them that when they did, they were getting a 'square meal'. Everyone laughed. The boys saw a lot of rope on board and wondered how much there actually was.

Sailor 1, "There are about 25 miles of rope on the ship. Periodically, they need to be replaced. We buy rope right here on this pier. That is one of the industries you have in Boston and there are a lot of people working at rope making. I do not know if you boys realize it or not, but shipbuilding is also a big industry in Boston."

The boys admitted that was new to them. They told the sailors they were farm boys, and this was their first time coming to the wharf. The sailors eventually had other things that required their attention, so they departed. Joshua and Caleb then retraced their steps back through the narrow streets.

They ended up in the common area of Boston. It was an open area of land with trees and grazing areas for animals. In a different time, this area would be a gathering place for large meetings, public festivals, and a possible hanging of a convicted criminal. Joshua watched the people coming and going while Caleb explored the area. It seemed like most of them were Soldiers. They had taken over much of the common ground and pitched tents for shelter. They walked around as if they owned the place. At one point, a group of soldiers literally almost trampled over Joshua. One of them angrily demanded that Joshua watch where he was going. He forcefully shoved Joshua, and he almost fell to the ground. Joshua bristled at that. Had he been older, bigger and stronger, he might have challenged that mouthy soldier. Fortunately, he was not. A townsman, seeing the incident came over to make sure he was alright. He was not hurt, but he was angry. He had not done anything wrong. The soldier ran into him, not the other way around.

"I know how you feel, boy," the townsman responded, "I feel the same way sometimes. These British redcoats seem to think they own everything, and the sun, moon, and stars revolve around them. A lot of us here are getting more and more disgusted with this heavy-handed treatment from our so-called 'benevolent' king."

That was Joshua's first introduction to the redcoat British soldiers. He also was now a personal witness of the British overreach. He did not like it. Joshua's anger cooled down and he began again to observe the other people in the area; the ones that were supposed to be there. There seemed to be all kinds, obvious sailors, some common laborers, and some that seemed... well more like aristocrats. Their dress was different than the sailors or the laborers or even his own dress. The men wore suits, and the ladies wore long intricately fashioned dresses often in bright colors. Joshua was intrigued.

After a bit, a younger female caught his eye. She appeared much older than she probably was. Her apparel seemed to elevate her status. Joshua had been around girls; after all he and Caleb both had sisters. This one, though, was different. Her dress was exquisite. Her matching coat neatly covered the top of the dress. Her hair was not the usual wild strands he was used to on his sisters. It was elegantly woven about her head with a small perfectly positioned hat on top. Her auburn hair glistened in the sunlight. He could not take his eyes off her. He was sure his heart had skipped a beat when he first saw her...

Calab returned to Joshua while he was still enthralled by her and woke him from his revery.

Caleb noticing Joshua's fixation, "What are you staring at? Oh, wait a minute, I see. Hey! She is pretty!"

"Ah, yeah. I guess she is," Joshua responded.

"Do you know who she is?" asked Caleb.

Joshua answered, "No"

Caleb prodded Joshua," Why don't you go over and talk to her?"

Joshua flushed, "No, no, she is with her family, and it would not be right to impose."

"You would like to, though, wouldn't you? " Caleb chided.

Joshua did not answer him. He just turned away. They began walking toward home but then got an urge to look back again before she was out of sight.

He saw her looking back at him. She had a curious yet puzzled look on her face. Joshua flushed deep red and quickly turned around, running past Caleb.

Caleb was startled, "Hey, wait for me, Josh."

***

The animosity between the Loyalists and the Patriots was increased each year as the British tried to force compliance to the new laws. The arguments became more heated in the towns. Two years after Joshua and Caleb went to Boston, a British warship patrolling for smugglers ran aground in Rhode Island. A local mob burned the ship and then were accused of treason. [3] The next year a Tea Act was passed in which the British imposed special taxes designed to undercut the price of the smuggler's tea. A large group of men including the Sons of Liberty led by Samuel Adams then fifty-one and John Hancock then thirty-six dressed as Native American Indians threw over three hundred chests of tea into the sea. Their slogan was:

"No Taxation Without Representation."[4]

John Adams was pleased. George Washington who had led troops in the French and Indian War strongly disapproved. Another leader by the name of Benjamin Franklin insisted that the East India Tea Company be reimbursed for their loss. There were people on both sides, some praising the act of defiance and others condemning it. Six months later the British tried to close the port of Boston with the Boston Port Act. The talk got even more heated.

Some said: "Those that destroyed the property of the tea company should be punished!"

Others said: "Even if you believe that the perpetrators should be pun-

---

3. Wikipedia, Gaspee Affair

4. Wikipedia, Boston Tea Party

ished, why should the whole town of Boston be punished for the lawless acts of a few? That is a flagrant attack on individual rights! It is not fair!"

Joshua and Caleb became curious about the Boston Tea party event and wanted to see the actual site. He and Caleb finished their chores one day and headed for Boston. They were excited to see the harbor again, especially Caleb. Joshua had another reason for going. They arrived at the harbor and looked over the water. They tried to envision water turning brown filled with tea. They imagined the rebels dressed as Indians doing the deed. It was almost like reenacting some of their childhood fantasies in which they participated in fighting an enemy. This time it wasn't the Indians.

Caleb wanted to see everything. Joshua was distracted. He kept looking around, hoping to see that girl. He had been enchanted and never forgot her, even though several years had passed. He wondered what she looked like now. Did she still look as beautiful as he remembered her? Was she married, after all girls in the colonies often marry as young as fifteen? They walked around a little longer and then decided to head back home before it got too late. It was winter and the sun went down early. On the way out, they passed a dry goods store near the waterfront. Suddenly Joshua, deep in thought and not watching where he was going, bumped into someone. He quickly apologized to the person as he turned around. It was that girl! He knew her instantly and was dumbstruck. She scolded him for not watching where he was going and then stopped quickly facing him.

Their eyes met.

"You're that boy"

Joshua could only fumble a few "ahs and us"

"Who are you?" She asked. "I saw you staring at me right here several years ago. Why did you do that? Why were you staring? Why did you run into me like that?

Joshua hung his head. She realized he was embarrassed and let up a little. Girl in a softer tone, "What is your name?"

Joshua responded, "Joshua, Joshua Rutledge." He quickly added: "I am sorry I walked into you; I hope you were not hurt."

"No," she said then with a curious look on her face and asked the same question she had asked before, "Why were you staring at me the last time?"

A flustered Joshua responded, "I was younger and had never seen such a beautiful girl before and I..."

He did not know what to say. He was not used to talking to girls other than his and Caleb's sisters.

She was secretly enthralled but tried not to let it show. She raised her head a bit in a proper lady-like stance.

"You know it is not polite to stare!" She scolded.

Joshua hung his head, "I am sorry, I did not mean to stare. I..I.."

She was even more drawn to this shy but incredibly handsome young man. She decided to let him off the hook.

"I forgive you. My name is Jessica, Jessica Pitman."

"I am pleased to meet you, Jessica Pitman."

"And I likewise, Joshua"

She purposely did not use his last name as a signal that he could now be a little less formal with her.

Jessica was curious, "Why have you come to the wharf today?"

Joshua not wanting to reveal his real reason for coming responded, "My friend, Caleb and I came into town to see where the rebels had participated in the tea party."

Caleb had been watching this interaction quietly from the side wondering where this encounter was leading. Joshua realized he was standing there and quickly introduced him to Jessica. Jessica acknowledged Caleb.

"My family and I do not hold with that act of wonton destruction of private property. It was wrong of those rebels to do that. My father is a merchant and has a store here. We do not take kindly to having our property destroyed." Jessica insisted.

Joshua realized he was talking to someone with more Loyalist leanings. His family was more inclined to side with the Sons of Liberty, so he held his peace. He simply agreed with her on the destruction of property and let it go at that. Caleb wanted to defend the rebel action as justified because of all the heavy-handed acts of Britain against the colonies. Joshua quickly restrained him with a hard look. Caleb saw it and shut up. Joshua tried to say something more to her but just then her father came out of the store.

"There is my father."

Her father came over to them with a questioning face as to who his daughter was talking to. Jessica quickly read his thought.

Jessica looking at her father and then the young men, "Father, I would like to introduce you to Joshua and Caleb. I just met them. We have been having a friendly conversation here while I was waiting for you."

Joshua and then Caleb held out their hands to her father. He shook them.

"What brings you to Boston? You do not appear to live around here."

Joshua responded, "We just came in to see where all the excitement happened in the harbor, just curiosity. Our families are farmers a little way outside of town."

"Hmmm, a bad event for sure. The King will not be pleased with those rebel acts. It will not go well for the colonies if these acts keep happening. Well, Jessica, we need to be going. Say goodbye to your new acquaintances and let us begone. Good day gentlemen."

He then walked off. Jessica obeyed her father and said goodbye.

"I hope I will see you again, Joshua," Jessica said softly.

Encouraged, Joshua responded, "Me too."

She smiled as she turned away. Joshua did not see it. This handsome young man intrigued her. Caleb could not resist kidding Joshua.

"I think Joshua is in love," teased Caleb.

Joshua brushing him away, "I just met the girl!"

"Is that the same girl you saw some years ago?" Caleb asked.

A flustered Joshua answered, "Well yeah But.."

Caleb wasn't buying it, "Okay..." as if to say you are not fooling me, I know you too well. He then added, "She is even prettier than I remember."

They then headed home. Joshua knew; however, he would try to see her again.

The British added three more rulings in May that year that infuriated the colonists:

The Massachusetts Government Act repealed the colonies charter replacing the elected local government with an appointed one.

The Administration Justice Act which moved trials involving British officials charged with capital offenses to England or another colony.

The new Quartering Act permitted the requisition of unoccupied buildings for quartering soldiers.

Even the Loyalists, while still loyal to England, were dismayed at the harsh treatment by Britain. War was coming. Even as the first skirmishes were being fought, the Loyalists preserved a hope that they could restore fellowship with King George III and England.

One Loyalist insisted, "The colonies should appeal to King George like a child that has been hurt by his parent and wishes to restore the parent-child relationship."

The Loyalists convinced Congress to send an Olive Branch petition to King George the following year.

It was signed by John Hancock and almost all those who would later sign the Declaration of Independence. King George III flatly refused. By then, war had already begun.

***

Joshua was even more smitten by Jessica and wanted to see her again. He decided he would go to her father's store on the pretext of buying supplies for the family. The next time his parents needed something, he volunteered to go. His parents were pleased with his willingness but a little puzzled that he volunteered so quickly. They let it go and sent him out. Thomas had a horse drawn wagon for use on the farm. Joshua quickly cleaned it up, hitched up the horse, and went off. Elizabeth pondered the actions of her son. It was not like him to be so meticulous. She made a mental note to talk with him when he returned, especially since he seemed to go to extra lengths to clean up and dress his best.

Elizabeth thought, "What is up with him?"

Joshua made it into town a little before noon, found the store and went in. He was pleased to see Jessica behind the counter apparently serving customers. When she saw him, she nodded in acknowledgement, finished serving a customer, and walked over to greet him.

"Hello, Joshua."

Joshua responding uncomfortably, "hello."

"What brings you into town this day."

"I came to buy some supplies for our family." Joshua did not tell her the whole truth.

"Good, I will help you personally. What do you need?"

"Some sugar….Mom gave me a list."

She told him to give it to her, and she would collect the items.

After retrieving the supplies she asked, "Was that all you came in for?"

He flushed and fumbled for something to say. She turned around so that he would not see the smile on her face. She instantly knew the answer to her question. The thought warmed and energized her. She recalled something her aunt always said while she was growing up.

"A woman is never more powerful than when she stands as a helpmate beside her man."

She had no idea why that thought crossed her mind. Joshua wasn't her man. She had just met him a few weeks ago! He is handsome, strong and those pretty blue eyes... well they were gorgeous. He wasn't her man though. She pushed the thoughts out of her mind and went about gathering the items on the list.

Jessica asked, "How will you pay for these items?"

Joshua responded, "I have some tobacco leaves that I believe are worth something."

"Ok, I will need to see what you have and then I can tell you what we will offer you for them," Jessica replied.

The two of them went out of the store to the wagon so he could show her the leaves.

"These look pretty good. Bring them in so we can weigh them."

He did so. She came back with a price which sounded fair, so he accepted. The amount was a little higher than the value of the goods he had asked for. "Would you like the difference in English coin, or should we give you a credit for a future purchase?" Jessica asked.

"Credit." And then quickly added: "I think my parents would prefer the credit."

He did not actually know that. It just gave him an excuse to come back. Jessica flushed slightly. She knew it was because he wanted to come back. Joshua was about to leave; he could not think of anything else to say to her.

Jessica realizing Joshua wanted to spend more time with her responded, "It is almost lunch time, and I have brought much more food than I can eat. Would you like to join me? We have a little sitting area on the side of the store."

He was enchanted and could not suppress the smile.

Jessica read his mind, "That settles it, come with me."

She turned to another clerk in the store and said something about a lunch break. She then turned away from him and walked toward the door with a slight smile on her face. He dutifully followed her out to the sitting area. They talked for quite a while. She liked the initial control, but her compassionate side warmed up to him when he spoke of his family, his faith, and his experiences. A little prodding and he might open up. When they finally parted, her aunt's saying reappeared in her mind. She knew that she wanted to see Joshua again. He wanted to see her too. In the months that followed, they had several "lunches" together. When he returned home, he was beaming. Elizabeth saw it and knew the answer to her question when he left. Joshua has found a girl! She would extract the details from him later as only a mother can do. For now, she just pondered it and left him alone.

***

A week later, after Elizabeth had talked with her son and found out more about this girl, Jessica, she nudged her husband to have the "talk" with Joshua. Thomas was surprised.

"Did he say something to you?" asked Thomas.

"Haven't you noticed him around here? He is getting dressed up all to go into town. He even cleaned the wagon!" Elizabeth responded indignantly.

Thomas frowned, "So?"

"Thomas are you blind? Our son has found a girl he likes."

"Are you sure?" doubting her conclusion.

Elizabeth explained sternly, "Of course. I got it out of him last week. Her name is Jessica, and she is the daughter of a shop owner in town. Now do your duty as his father and have that talk!"

Thomas relented, "Yes dear."

Thomas thought about it for a couple of days. He wanted to think through what he should say to his son. He knew the Bible told him to "train up a child in the way he should go." [5] That was part of his responsibility under God as a father. The next day he asked if he could talk to Joshua.

Joshua responded, "Sure!"

Thomas began, "Josh, your mom has told me that you have met a girl."

Joshua a bit confused as to where this was going, "Yeah, Dad, no big deal"

"Do you like her?" asked Thomas.

"Yeah, I do, a lot."

"Well, son, that's ok, I just want to have a little talk with you about

---

5. Proverbs 22:6

things."

"Dad, I already know about such things. Come on, we live on a farm. There have been a lot of births here. I know where babies come from."

"I am sure you do. That isn't quite what I wanted to talk to you about."

Joshua was puzzled but willing to listen, "Ok."

Thomas settling into his best lecture voice, "Son, you are entering a time when your mom and I expect you to choose a mate. It is a wonderful time, an exciting time, but it is also a dangerous time. It is the time that Satan will attack you to deceive you like never before."

Joshua answered, "Dad, Jessica and I are just friends."

Thomas insisting on continuing, "I know but hear me out. Courtship begins with friendship which then can grow into something deeper and richer, marriage. I assume you want at some point want to be married?"

"Well yes, but.."

Thomas wishing to bring in the Bible to support what he was saying, "Did you know that God performed the first marriage? He said in the book of Genesis that it was not good that man should be alone and then he made a helpmate for Adam. Her name was Eve. She was the perfect mate for Adam. She was made from one of his ribs, symbolizing that she would walk beside him for the rest of his life. She was not to be his boss; she was to be his companion, his friend, his counselor, his partner, his helpmate. Josh, why do you think God instituted marriage?"

Joshua was silent, he had not thought about it.

Thomas continued, "Josh, the main purpose for marriage is procreation and protection of children. Of course, sex is involved, and that is very pleasurable, but that is not the main purpose. Children are the main purpose. You and your brothers and sisters came into the world without the ability to protect yourselves, clothe yourselves, feed yourselves, or even discern for yourselves how to live and function in the world. Your mother and

I had the responsibility to protect, provide, teach, and nurture you to a point where you could become good citizens in this world. It is not an easy job, and so God set the example with Adam and Eve. He brought Adam a helpmate. It is a two-person job. It is extremely hard to do it alone. Even in nature God brought animals together a male and a female often for life and they nurtured new life together. Your mother and I are not perfect, nobody is, but we have tried to do the best that we could."

"Dad, I think you and mom have done a great job. I love you both."

"Thank you for saying that Josh. Here is the point, though, God has provided an extremely pleasurable activity that is part of the process, sex. God also warned that sex was only to be engaged by married people. One of the Ten Commandments says: 'Thou shalt not commit adultery.'[6] Other passages indicate that pre-marital sex is also forbidden. Many people have ignored those warnings, and Satan has used that rebellion to undermine marriages."

Joshua wishing the lecture to end, "Dad, I know these things, I have heard them from you and mom and our Pastor."

"Josh, I am not telling you not to pursue a relationship with Jessica. I am telling you to guard and protect the relationship because she may be your future mate. Please listen and ponder the words I have told you. Ask God for insight."

Joshua realizing his father had his best interest at heart responded, "I will."

The two hugged each other and they parted.

---

6. Exodus 20:14

Chapter 3

Boil Over

The first governor of Virginia, a man by the name of Patrick Henry, on March 23, 1775, in a speech in Richmond, Virginia declared:

"Gentlemen may cry, 'Peace, Peace,' but there is no peace. The war is actually begun! The next gale that sweeps from the north will bring to our ears the clash of resounding arms! Our brethren are already in the field! Why stand we here idle? ... Is life so dear, or peace so sweet, as to be purchased at the price of chains and slavery? Forbid it, Almighty God! I know not what course others may take; but as for me, give me liberty, or give me death!"[1]

On April 18, 1775, the Sons of Liberty members Paul Revere and William Dawes rode to warn the Patriots the British were coming. They alerted up to forty other patriots. [2] The next day the British moved on Lexington and then Concord to disarm the colonists. The story was that there were hundreds of British soldiers at Lexington against the less than one hundred militiamen gathered on the town green.

The British Major shouted, "Throw down your arms! Ye villains, ye Rebels."

---

1. History, Patrick Henry, by: History.com Editors

2. History, The Midnight Ride of William Dawes

Some accounts indicate that the militiamen were ordered to stand their ground, others indicate they were ordered at the last minute to disperse. Someone fired a shot, and the battle ensued. When the smoke cleared, eight militiamen were dead, about the same number wounded. There was only one redcoat reported wounded. The British soldiers sought out arms but did not find many. They burned what they found. The fire got a little out of control which convinced the militiamen that Concord was now being targeted. They ran to Concord's north bridge, defended by some British soldiers. The British soldiers were pushed back. Later reports declared that one of these shots was the "shot heard 'round the world". The British spent several hours searching around Concord and then return to Boston. The colonists by this time had prepared for this. There were militiamen known as minutemen who had been recruited to gather at moment's notice in case of attack. About two thousand arrived in Boston before the British soldiers returned.

There were other events as well. Ethan Allen and the Green Mountain Boys seized Fort Ticonderoga in the north. [3] Even though Boston and the surrounding area were the initial focus of the war, this relatively small battle would later prove to be instrumental in gaining victory against the British in Boston.

The Second Continental Congress formalized the Patriot militias into a Continental Army to be led by George Washington. Before Washington was even able to assume command, the Battle of Bunker Hill in Boston occurred.

The city of Boston was on a Peninsula with a narrow land entrance to the southwest, the rest was surrounded by water. There was also another

---

3. American Battlefield Trust Fort Ticonderoga (1775)

peninsula across the water to the north which also was considered part of Boston. The British were in complete control of all water access and lay siege to the city.

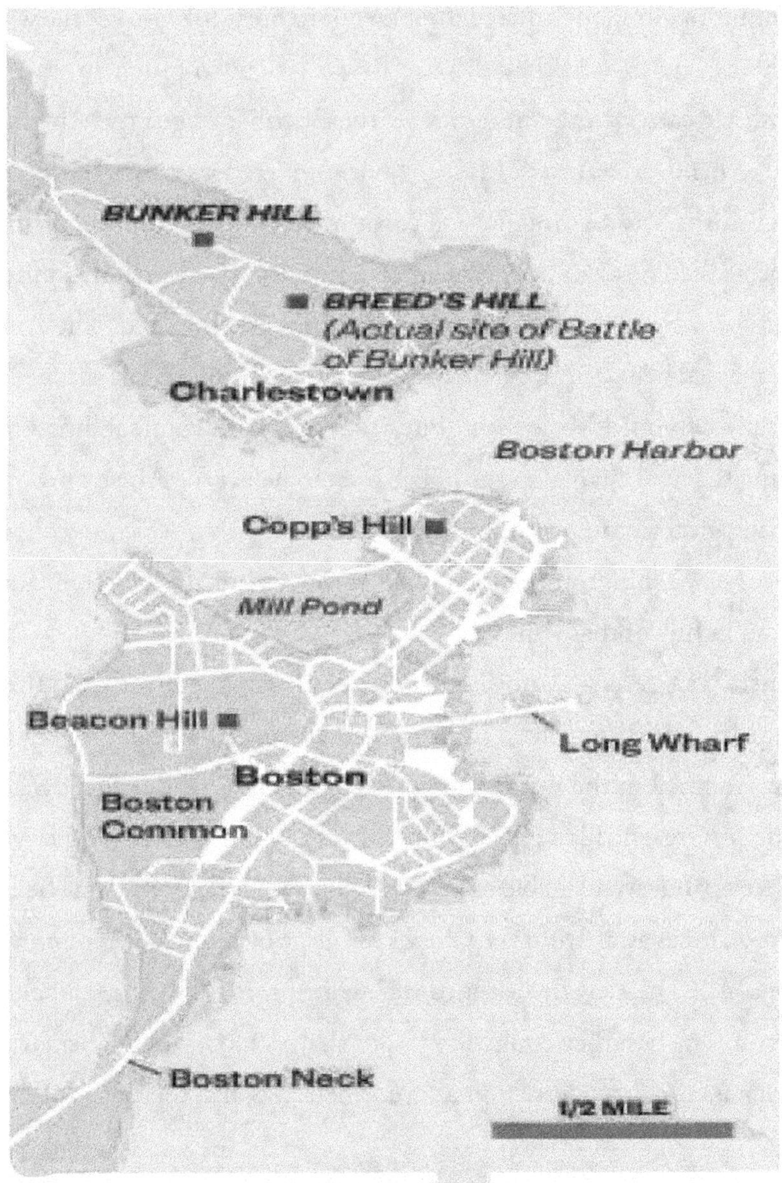

Boston and Bunker Hill Area

The American forces under Colonel William Prescott built up fortifications on top of Breed's Hill (near Bunker Hill) on the second peninsula. Initially, they wanted to fortify Bunker Hill but chose instead Breed's Hill. They were attacked by over two thousand British troops. To conserve ammunition, Prescott ordered the men not to fire until you see "the whites of their eyes." When they did fire it was lethal; so much so, that the British retreated. In the next charge, the British engaged the Americans hand to hand. The Americans being outnumbered were forced to retreat. The British victory, though, was costly with over one thousand British soldiers killed or wounded. The reported statistics said that one hundred Americans were killed, and three hundred others wounded. The Americans avoided being captured because Peter Salem, a Black soldier, shot and mortally wounded Major John Pitcairn, the British commanding officer leading the final charge up the hill. [4] Even in defeat the Americans won a psychological victory.

George Washington then assumed command of the army outside of Boston in July of that same year.

There were several skirmishes reported between the British and the Patriots some widely separated from each other. The Americans, for example took Montreal in the north and later a battle in Quebec. There was the Battle of Great Bridge in Virginia. Further south patriots laid siege to Ninety-Six but were unable to take it. Folklore says it got its name because it was 96 miles away from the Cherokee village of Keowee (later known as Clemson)). The cleverly designed star-shaped fort proved too difficult to overrun. The best they could do was put sharp shooters on higher ground and harass the defenders from above. There was also the Battle of Great

---

4. American Battlefield Trust, Peter Salem

Cane Break in South Carolina. [5]

The Continental army was a ragtag composite of smaller militias. The men signed on to fight for short periods of time. Most of the men were farmers and when it came to harvest time, they desired to go back and work their farms. Washington understood the predicament; they had families to support. Their livelihood was wrapped up in the farm. It also meant that they did not wish to venture too far from home. The northern militias did not want to fight in the south and the southern militias did not want to fight in the north. It had to be a nightmare for Washington to figure out just what troops he could use in any given battle. Even harder to coordinate the efforts between separate militias led by their favorite leaders. In many cases, not only the head of the household came to fight but also older sons. When the time came to leave, the army was severely depleted with soldiers. It was said that Washington had no more than twenty thousand soldiers at any one time, yet there may have been over two-hundred-thousand men that enlisted. The army was poorly equipped, short on supplies, and rarely paid. When it got really bad, it was said that Washington himself pulled from his own resources to pay for needed supplies. [6]

Meanwhile, the British governor of Virginia issued a proclamation offering freedom to any slaves of rebellious Americans to fight on the British side. Thousands of slaves responded. A little later, the Patriots made the same offer to fight with the Continental army. At one time, almost ten percent of Washington's forces consisted of Black soldiers. [7]

---

5. American Battlefield Trust, Ninety-Six, Siege of Ninety Six

6. American Battlefield Trust 10 Facts: The Continental Army

7. Ibid

There were also many loyalists that took up arms for the British feeling they were British citizens and needed to put down the rebellion against the British crown. The fight was no longer a fight between Americans and the British; it was now as much a civil war as a fight against the British crown. The British were not used to fighting against the "hit and run tactics" of the Colonists. British soldiers felt the tactics were cowardly and they did not respect the Continental army. The British soldiers even resurrected a song originally written about 1755 mocking the colonial soldiers called "Yankee Doodle".

Yankee Doodle

Yankee Doodle went to town
A-riding on a pony,
Stuck a feather in his cap
And called it macaroni.

(Chorus)
Yankee Doodle keep it up,
Yankee Doodle dandy,
Mind the music and the step,
And with the girls be handy.

Father and I went down to camp,
Along with Captain Gooding,
And there we saw the men and boys
As thick as hasty pudding.

The word "doodle" was based on the German word 'deudal' meaning dummy. The British had hired many Hessians mercenaries over time to fight for them, and they may have been involved in the origin of the song. "Macaroni" was kind of a slang expression for the hair pieces that the British and some colonial aristocrats wore. The curly hair resembled macaroni. The British were jesting that these dumb colonists would put a feather in their cap and that made them aristocrats. The song was meant as a taunt against the colonial soldiers. The Continental army threw it back at the British soldiers by learning the song, adding fife and drum and played it throughout the Revolutionary war. The British later regretted ever creating the song![8]

There also was another phenomenon in the Continental army, a significant number of women were present. When some of the men went to war, the women that would be left behind may not have felt they could keep up with the farm. In those cases, they joined with their husbands. They served the troops. They served as cooks, menders, or in other noncombative areas. [9]

The Continental army in the beginning had no navy. The British were in complete control of the sea. They could blockade wherever they wished and prevent needed supplies, weapons, and ammunition from reaching the army. Washington realized he needed some sort of naval presence and convinced the Continental Congress to fund some naval ships. It would take too long to build them, however, so some were pressed into service from private owners. Five were obtained, all of them were schooners and

---

8. Wikipedia, Yankee Doodle

9. American Battlefield Trust, Women in the American Revolution

they were outfitted with some guns.[10] The leaders took a lesson from the smugglers who brought tea and other goods, almost all were using schooners of various sizes. These were much more maneuverable than the larger British warships and could be brought into shallower water where the warships could not go. Smugglers had learned that lesson a long time ago.

The schooners were no match for the big guns and large number of guns on the warships in a broadside to-broadside battle. They could, however, sail in on an angle, avoiding a direct broadside, fire their guns, and harass the warships. If the warship got too aggressive and tried to attack, they would head for shallower water. The technique proved to be successful with some of the more daring captains. The Continental Navy was able to capture some ships. The supplies and guns aboard provided a welcome relief for Washingtons beleaguered army.

When winter came in full force, battles subsided. Neither the Americans nor the British liked to fight in the cold of winter. Of course it was different in the warm Bahamas. The Newly created Continental Navy were successful in a raid on Nassau, Bahamas, another English territory, in March. [11] Not a big deal as there were few defenders but a win for the Americans was a win. The British were way too strong at sea. They could move large numbers of troops and supplies in at will. Meanwhile, Washington and his army had to scramble for supplies and had to march everywhere, both of which took a toll on his men. He needed a way to get additional supplies. He needed a psychological boost for morale. He needed some naval successes.

---

10. Wikipedia, Continental Navy

11. American Revolutionary War, Battle of Nassau

***

The biggest event that winter was not a battle, but the publishing of a pamphlet signed "Common Sense". It was later determined that it was written by Thomas Paine. Copies of the pamphlet were distributed and read throughout the colonies. Joshua obtained a copy in one of his trips to see Jessica. He read it and wanted to share and discuss it with his family. The following Sunday after church, the Rutledge's and the Reed's gathered together at the Reed home to share a meal. Their home was a little larger than the Rutledge home with a bigger main room. After they had eaten, Joshua wanted to read the whole pamphlet aloud, but Elizabeth convinced him to just read the main ideas. He complied. The pamphlet was entitled: "On the Origin and Design of Government in General' with Concise Remarks on the English Constitution."

Joshua explained, "This pamphlet says some pretty strong things about government. For example, he says early in it: 'Society is produced by our wants and government by our wickedness'. Later he says: 'Society in every state is a blessing, but government, even in its best state, is but a necessary evil.' Further on he says: 'Government, like dress, is a badge of lost innocence; the palaces of kings are built upon the ruins of the bowers of paradise.'"

"Sounds like he has read his Bible." Elizabeth interjected.

Thomas agreed, "He seems to be familiar with the story of Adam and Eve where mankind lost innocence by disobeying God's commandment not to eat of the knowledge of good and evil."

"That is interesting." John joined in and then added, "Didn't Pastor

Josiah say recently something like: 'If God and Angels were in charge, we would not need government, but because man does not let God be in charge, we have to have government.'"

"I remember that!" Mary exclaimed. "I found that really inciteful. It really got me to thinking about how all mankind are sinners. There is none righteous, no not one and why we needed a redeemer, why Jesus had to come and die for our sins."

Some of the younger children started asking some questions and there was some back-and-forth answers and more questions and more answers.

Caleb became curious, "Josh, what else does he say?"

"He goes on to say that when people are attached to each other, they can work things out, but when there are more immigrants there is as he says: 'the necessity of establishing some form of government to supply the defect in moral virtue.'"

Joshua could see that his mother was getting a little impatient, so he scanned the pamphlet to summarize what the author was saying.

"He then goes on to say something about as populations increase there has to be a representative form of government instead of a pure democracy but whatever form, the simpler it is the better."

The children kept interrupting, so Elizabeth told them to remember their questions and she would sit down with them later and explain it all. Right now, though, she asked that they be quiet and listen and let Joshua finish.

Joshua continued, "In the next part, he attacks the English Constitution. He compares the king to a tyrant and there is an aristocratical tyranny as well. He thinks that the elected persons of the Commons are not strong enough to check the power of the other two."

"Wow, that is pretty strong," Thomas exclaimed, "and here in the colonies we do not even have representation in the Parliament to check the power of the king."

Mary questioned," Wasn't that part of the slogan during the Boston Tea Party?"

Caleb answered, "Yeah, No taxation without representation"

What did they mean by that slogan?" Mary asked.

Joshua answered, "The British were treating us like we were conquered enemies instead of British citizens. British citizens have the right to send representatives to Parliament to represent them and have a say in government decisions including taxation. We are being taxed, though, without any say in the matter. Patriots felt that was wrong."

Sarah who had been listening joined in, "Do you agree?"

Joshua answered, "Yes."

Later, he says that in the beginning there were no kings" Johua explained, "and 'the consequence of which was, there were no wars; it is the pride of kings which throws mankind into confusion."

"There is something to that," Caleb added, "look at just what we have seen in our lives. What else does he say, Josh?"

Joshua continued, "As the exalting one man above the rest cannot be justified on the equal rights of nature, so neither can it be defended on the authority of scripture; for the will of the almighty as declared by Gideon and the prophet Samuel, expressly disapproves of government by kings."

"I do not think he will gain much favor with King George with that statement!" John exclaimed.

Elizabeth agreed, "You can say that again!"

Joshua continued, "He is radical. He doesn't stop there. A little further on he appears to be attacking the Anglican and Catholic churches. He says: 'there is much of kingcraft as priestcraft in withholding the scripture from the public in popish countries."

Isn't that why a lot of people came to America," Caleb asked, "to escape

being told what to believe by the church and to read the Bible for themselves?"

"Absolutely, Caleb." replied Thomas. "The Puritans are a good example.
They first tried to point out the errors in the church and purify it. When
they could not, a group of them left everything and came here. Many
died just so they could have religious freedom to worship as they chose not
as someone else dictates. There were others too, the Quakers, Lutherans,
Presbyterians "

Joshua added. "He also comes down on hereditary succession. He says:

*'For all men being originally equals, no one by birth could have a right
to set up his own family in perpetual preference to all others forever,' and
then adds: 'and though himself might deserve some decent degree of honors of
his contemporaries, yet his descendants might be far too unworthy to inherit
them.'"*

"I think I agree with this man." John joined in.

"I am reminded of the Bible priest in I Samuel named Eli who had two
worthless sons, Hophni and Phinehas. There was also Solomon the wisest
king who had very unwise offspring."

"He makes a strong case," interjected Thomas, "but I do not think the
British or the Loyalist's here will take kindly to him."

Joshua a little more emphatically, "You must hear this last paragraph:

*'In England a king hath little more to do than to make war and give away
places, which, in plain terms, is to impoverish the nation and set it together
by the ears. A pretty business indeed for a man to be allowed eight hundred
thousand sterling a year for and worshipped into the bargain! Of more worth
is one honest man to society, and in the sight of God than all the crowned
ruffians that ever lived...'"*

"Hear hear!" Shouted John. "If I was a drinking man, I would be raising
a pint to that last statement!"

"You better not be a drinking man!" Mary inserted sternly.

John just looked at her and smiled. After the presentation, some of the others wanted to read some of it for themselves. The younger children became a little bored and wanted to do something else.

Sarah, Caleb's younger sister (she was 3 years younger) came over to Joshua.

Sarah touched Joshua's arm, "Wow Josh, you really know a lot. I was impressed by your ability to condense and summarize that Common Sense pamphlet."

"Thank you, Sarah." he replied. "It was kind of you to say that."

Sarah blushed, "I have always known that you were smart, Josh."

All the Rutledge and Reed children had grown up together, played together, went to church together, and kidded each other. Somehow, Joshua sensed something different about Sarah he had not noticed before. She seemed... older, more mature... She smiled at him, put her hand on his arm again, and it felt good. There was something different about her...

Sarah left her hand on his arm for a moment more, then turned and walked away. She liked Joshua. She was now fourteen, almost fifteen. She had filled out more, her hips were a little bigger, her breasts were more noticeable. She hoped Joshua would take more notice of her. Secretly she dreamed of Joshua and her together more than just family friends.

The families talked and fellowshipped a little more. Then Thomas, Elizabeth, and their children begged leave of the Reed's so they could get back home before dark. There was not a lot of talk on the way. The younger children were tired. Thomas, Elizabeth, and the older children were deep in thought. They were pondering this Common-Sense pamphlet. Joshua and Caleb were considering what they needed to do about it.

***

Toward the end of February 1776, Elizabeth decided to make her way into town to obtain some supplies. Snow was still on the ground, and it was cold, but the weather was clear. She bundled herself up and took the horse and wagon. Along the way, she spotted something off the side of the road. She couldn't see what it was until she got close. It appeared to be a young girl or woman lying on the ground under a tree. Thinking she may be hurt; she stopped and went over to her. She became even more concerned when she noticed a lot of blood around her legs. When she came up to her, Elizabeth was horrified. The girl was holding a bloody metal hook. She had thrust the hook up inside her and what she pulled out lay on the snow between her legs. Elizabeth stood in shock; there was in the burst open sack the remains of a child. It was tiny, probably only three to four months along in the pregnancy. Elizabeth could see every feature, the head, body, arms, legs. One arm had been ripped off and lay separated from the rest. Elizabeth's face must have expressed the horror of the scene so vividly that the girl, who had been staring up at Elizabeth, quickly turned away and lowered her head.

Elizabeth sternly with tears in her eyes, "What have you done!"

The girl did not answer. She just hung her head.

Elizabeth pulled a piece of cloth from her pocket and gently picked up the remains of the child. She cleaned it the best that she could and wrapped it in cloth. At that point she sobbed heavily. It was just too much for her to bear. She remembered how she felt when she and Thomas lost their daughter, Sarah. She had felt Sarah inside her. She remembered sensing when Sarah was upset. She would talk to her, and she knew that Sarah heard every word. Somehow Elizabeth's voice seemed to calm her. All these memories flooded back to Elizabeth. Then came the sickness. Sarah was a beautiful child, almost one year old. She was sick for a week with her life slowly ebbing away. Then she breathed her last breath. It had been too much for Elizabeth. Thomas had to hold her tightly to him, even as she flailed angrily at him.

Elizabeth thought, "Why would God allow this?"

There was no answer, of course; God's ways are far above man's ways, and He is not obligated to explain everything to all of us. All those emotions now flooded back through her mind as she held the remnants of this tiny child. She must have expressed every emotion on her face because the young girl was now sobbing in total despair at what she had done.

Elizabeth's normal compassionate nature surfaced at this point, and she realized that this girl needed her help. She pushed the horror, outrage and anger aside. She looked closely at the girl and realized that she was still bleeding. She remembered the Bible teaching "Judge not that ye be not judged,"[12] and the story of the "Good Samaritan".[13] She remembered that she had been forgiven of her sins and that God could forgive even this young girl as well. She would need to talk the whole thing out with Thomas when she got home, but right now she needed to try to stop the bleeding and help this girl.

Elizabeth gently took hold of the girl's hand and she, still sobbing, looked back at her. Elizabeth's face had changed from horror and anger to gentle compassion. The girl could see it. She did what Elizabeth told her to do. Elizabeth asked her where she lived. She answered. Elizabeth helped

---

12. Matthew 7:1

13. Luke 10:30-36

her up, and they made their way back to the wagon.

Elizabeth then asked her if she wanted to bury her child (Elizabeth was still holding onto the cloth). The girl shook her head yes. Elizabeth found a tool in the wagon that she could use to get through the snow and dig in the frozen ground. She made a shallow grave and laid the remains in it. She bowed her head and said a short prayer. The two of them made their way to the girl's home. Elizabeth did not say anything to the girl's family, it was not her place. The girl thanked her, and Elizabeth left.

Later that evening, she relayed the entire story to Thomas. It was then that her emotions resurfaced.

An emotional Elizabeth asked, "How can any woman do that to her child?" Doesn't she realize that every child is a gift from God? How can a woman not feel that new life growing inside her and not be filled with love for that precious gift?"

"I do not know dear." Thomas replied. "We do not know what she has gone through or what led her to do such a terrible thing. We are not to judge."

Elizabeth answered, "I know, I know. It just seems so… incomprehensible that a mother would do such a thing. Even nature shows us how protective a mother is of her offspring. A bird will go to great lengths and even endanger herself to protect her eggs before they are hatched. Other animals do the same thing."

Thomas wishing to support his wife said, "You are right. I will hate to be anywhere near a momma bear if she thinks I am threatening her cubs!"

"Thomas," Elizabeth added in tears, "I held that little child in my hand. It was tiny but clearly human with little arms and legs and tiny fingers. How could she not protect her child?"

Thomas answered, "I do not know what possessed her to do such a terrible thing. I remember something that happened maybe two years ago when we had that fire in the small barn. Do you remember that fire?"

Elizabeth answered, "Yes!"

Thomas continued, 'When I went into the barn after the fire, I found a chicken in her nest. She was dead, roasted alive by the fire. It puzzled me why she did not escape. The door was open. When I lifted her up, I found seven eggs underneath her. Shortly after I did, the eggs began to hatch one at a time. We recovered six chicks out of the seven eggs. She had protected her offspring with her life!"

Elizabeth exclaimed, "Wow, I think I remember you telling me when it happened."

"I remember in Psalm 139 beginning in verse *14:*" *Thomas added.*

'I will praise thee, for I am fearfully and wonderfully made marvelous are thy works; and that my soul knoweth right well. My substance was not hid from thee, when I was made in secret, and curiously wrought in the lowest parts of the earth. Thine eyes did see my substance yet being unperfect; and in thy book all my members were written, which in continuance were fashioned, when as yet there was none of them.'"

Elizabeth puzzled, "You mean God could see us exactly like we would be when we were very tiny in the womb?"

Thomas answered, "I believe so, in fact I think he could see us right after conception."

"How can that be?"

Thomas: explained, "Well, builders can look at a set of plans for a very elaborate building and envision exactly what the building will look like when completed. Perhaps God puts something like that in the life cell."

"A tiny blueprint?" That surprised Elizabeth.

"Wow, I wonder what that would look like."

"I do not know," answered Thomas, "but maybe someday scientists will discover that blueprint and maybe God will even let them decipher it some. I think there may be blueprints for every living thing in His creation. I am guessing that they would be different than man's blueprint which might explain the emphasis that there are different "kinds" in the book of Genesis."

Elizabeth knowing Thomas's irritating habit of trying to add deeper explanations, "OK, smarty I know you are more intellectual than I am, but we don't have to go that deep."

Thomas accepting the rebuff, "Do you feel a little better now?"

Elizabeth answered, "A little, although, I still cannot understand how a woman would do such a thing. I hope that never becomes common place or something that woman think is their right especially before Almighty God. Thomas, that's worse than slavery. At least with slavery, slaves are allowed to live."

Chapter 4

Pushing Back

The colonists had enough of British soldiers trampling over their beloved Boston. They had fought well at Bunker Hill, even bloodied The British a whole lot more than the British expected, but they still had to retreat. They wanted their town back. Volunteers gathered on the outskirts of Boston not far from the Rutledge and Reed farms. They were angry and ready to fight. Washington was ready to lead them, but it would take some planning. If Washington was going to convince the British to leave, he needed some strategic firepower.

The British had enormous firepower. One British warship in the harbor had more cannon firepower than Washington had in his entire army. The British were strong masters of the sea. That is why they were able to successfully colonize lands in the Americas and halfway around the world. They were limited, though, in how far up the harbor they could go. There were shallow areas on the north side of Boston which could potentially cause the deep draft warships to run aground. They had to position themselves on the south seaward side of Boston instead of being able to surround the town. There was also a maneuverability problem for the British. There big guns on the lower deck of the ship were positioned for a broadside engagement. At sea, there is a lot of open water. The captain would maneuver the ship to bring the big guns to bear on their enemies.

Even then, only half the guns could engage, the ones on the side facing the enemy. If the captain wished to use the other guns, he would have to maneuver the ship around to bring them bear on the target.

In a harbor, the ship is limited by the boundaries of the harbor. The problem is compounded by the fact that the ships are driven by the wind and are at mercy of the wind direction. Shore cannons could be swung around to fire in wider array of angles. A good shore battery with fewer guns could be devastating. The British General Sir William Howe hoped to use the British ships in the harbor to neutralize the American guns.

Things did not go exactly as planned for the British. A storm foiled the British attempt to bring the superior British firepower on the Americans. In addition, Washington acquired a dozen canons in the successful Battle of Fort Ticonderoga. The Militia had been steadily moving them south towards Boston. Now it was time to put them into position south of Boston so they could engage the British shore battery and any warships that joined the fight. They had to do it quietly. General John Thomas with about eight hundred soldiers and over a thousand workers moved to fortify an area called Dorchester Heights. They needed a distraction to cover the sound they made while making the fortifications and moving the canons. Washington ordered another battery in a different location to open on the British on the outskirts of town. Once the Ticonderoga guns were in position and started firing, The British realized that they could no longer defend their position.[1]

Mid-March of 1776 saw thousands of British soldiers leaving Boston. The townspeople were jubilant! They had endured eight years of British

---

1. History, This Day in History, March 17, 1776, British Evacuate Boston

occupation of their town. Washington was a hero. Spirits were high. More volunteers poured in to join the Continental army. Joshua and Caleb decided to join too.

Joshua had to see Jessica one more time before he enlisted. He finished his chores as early as he could and then headed for her father's store. Fortunately, she was there and with a little prodding, he was able to persuade her to come out and talk to him. He waited in their usual place, mulling over in his mind what he would say. By this time, he knew he was deeply in love with Jessica and believed she loved him too. She had even told him she did, and he had told her that he loved her too. They were starting to think of a life together. Both knew that it would be hard to convince her father. He was not happy with the thought that his beautiful city belle would become a farmer's wife.

There was a class structure in the colonies. At the top were the big landowners. Next came the Merchants and the Clerics. Jessica and her family were in that class. The farmers were a step down from the merchants and clerics. Those landowners twenty-one and older could vote. Below them was the indentured servant, which is what Joshua's father had been for five years before acquiring the farm. Next, were the Indians and at the bottom were the slaves. It was generally frowned upon for anyone of a lower class to appear as though they belonged to a higher class. Slaves could be arrested, for example, if they wore the clothes of a merchant or large landowner. They were forbidden to do so. Most people knew that the Bible did not support such distinctions and were at times convicted by their conscience for holding to such things. Nevertheless, men being who they are, allowed classes to exist. Joshua knew he would have to overcome this class distinction. He was not prepared for an even more difficult barrier.

Jessica came out after a while and met him. She kissed him. It was a warm loving kiss. He was still enthralled with her and did not speak right away.

She had to pry a bit to get him to tell her why he wanted to talk with her.

A puzzled Jessica asked, "Joshua, what is so important that you had to talk with me?"

Joshua answered, "You know all the things that have been happening lately, the fighting, the British soldiers leaving Boston,"

Jessica a little apprehensive, "Okay..."

Joshua slowly continued, "Well, I have decided..."

He stopped to try to find the right words.

Jessica growing patient, "Come on Joshua, just talk to me."

Joshua after a lengthy pause, "I have decided to join the Continental army."

"You have what!?" Jessica shouted.

Joshua was not prepared for that response. He had never seen her like that. Her eyes glared at him, and he was shocked.

"Why would you do such a thing?" Jessica asked angrily, "You didn't even talk to me first. I thought we were a couple. Couple's share things, make decisions together."

She hurled a few more choice sentences at him, but he didn't quite get all of it, he was too shocked at her response.

"I am sorry, Jessica," he apologized, "I did not expect you would feel this way. We have talked about how wrong the British actions have been to all of us. I.. I thought you felt the same way."

"Same way, same way!" Jessica responded loudly, "You gave me no warning. What if you go off to fight and get killed? Did you ever think of that. How long is this thing going to last, a year, two, or a whole lot more? Am I supposed to just wait for you, all the time worrying about you?"

She turned around as if to walk away. Joshua could not think of what to do so he grabbed her and drew her close to him as if to protect her. Jessica loved his gentle touch and wanted to just melt in his arms; however, she had to maintain her angry façade. She already knew that Joshua was going to join the Continental Army and could read him like an open book. He had spoken many times of his anger against the British atrocities, and it was obvious that his heroes were the Sons of Liberty. It wasn't hard to deduce that at some point; he would join up.

She had her own things to tell Joshua and was struggling as to how to do it. Without knowing it, Joshua had given her the perfect solution. She would simply respond in anger to his decision. The truth was that she and her father were leaving Boston. If she told Joshua, she knew that he would do everything he could to persuade her to stay. She loved him, but she loved her father as well and did not want to have to decide between them. Her father was a Loyalist, and he feared that when the British soldiers left, his business would be destroyed by angry Patriots.

There had been other businesses that were attacked like the ones in the Boston Massacre or The Gaspee affair. He decided for his and his daughter's sake that they needed to leave. She was dreading telling Joshua but had decided to obey her father. She envisioned a huge conflict between the two of them and knew it would break her heart. She wasn't upset with Joshua for his decision; in fact, she admired him. She was concerned about his safety, of course. Joshua's decision gave her a means to break up with him. She would feign anger. She did not want to hurt Joshua but needed an excuse to separate from him for a few days. By the time he would come back to beg forgiveness for not including her in his decision, she would be gone. She hated deceiving him, but she dreaded even more the conflict between her father and him. She walked away appearing angry, but in fact was suffering from a broken heart.

Chapter 5

Declaration

Jessica, her father and brother left the following day on a ship bound for Nova Scotia. There were about a thousand loyalists that left on British ships. Her father left the store in the care of his brother who was a bit more sympathetic to the Patriot cause. He hoped by doing so that his store might be spared and someday he might return. While under sail, he could see that his daughter was very quiet. It was not like her. She was usually more exuberant. He tried to get her to open up to him as to what was wrong. He knew it was hard for her to leave her life in Boston and all her friends.

At first, she would not say anything. It wasn't until he mentioned Joshua that he knew he had uncovered the real reason for her sullenness. He guessed correctly that she was in love with him. He probed a bit more and she flooded him with her feelings. She told him how she hated to leave Joshua. She told him that Joshua was planning to join the Continental Army. She told him how she feigned anger when Joshua told her to cover up the fact that she was leaving and that it hurt her to do it. Jessica's father put his arms around her and held her as she began to cry. He told her he loved her and maybe God would somehow work things out.

***

That same year, 1776, a committee was appointed by the Continental Congress comprised of Thomas Jefferson, John Adams, and Benjamin Franklin to draft a document declaring the causes which impelled the colonies to separate from England. Thomas Jefferson, then thirty-three years old, produced the initial draft in two and half weeks. It was submitted, debated, a few edits were made, and then adopted by unanimous vote on July 4, 1776. Not all the members of Congress signed but of those who did about seventy percent were less than fifty years old, some even in their twenties. It began with a magnificent statement:

"WHEN in the Course of human events, it becomes necessary for one People to dissolve the Political Bands which have connected them with another, and to assume among the Powers of the Earth, the separate and equal Station to which the Laws of Nature and of Nature's God entitle them, a decent Respect to the Opinions of Mankind requires that they should declare the causes which impel them to the Separation.

WE hold these Truths to be self-evident, that all Men are created equal, that they are endowed by their Creator with certain un alienable Rights, that among these are Life, Liberty, and the Pursuit of Happiness- That to secure these Rights, Governments are instituted among Men, deriving their just Powers from the Consent of the Governed, that whenever any Form of Government becomes destructive of these Ends, it is the Right of the People to alter or to abolish it, and to institute new Government laying its Foundation on such Principles, and organizing its Powers in such Form, as to them shall seem most likely to effect their Safety and Happiness. Prudence indeed, will dictate that Governments long established should be changed for light and transient Causes;

and accordingly, all Experience hath shown, that Mankind are most disposed to suffer, while Evils are sufferable, then to right themselves by abolishing the Forms to which they are accustomed. But when a long Train of abuses and Usurpations, pursuing in variably the same Object, evinces a Design to reduce them under absolute Despotism, it is their Right, it is their Duty, to throw off such Government, and provide new Guards for their future Security. Such has been the patient Sufferance of these Colonies; and such is now the Necessity which constrains them to alter their former Systems of Government, The History of the present King of Great Britain is a history of repeated Injuries and Usurpations, all having in direct Object the Establishment of an absolute Tyranny over these States. To prove this, let Facts be submitted to a candid World."[1]

The latter part of the document lists all the "injuries and usurpations" that the Colonists had endured.

Copies were made of the document and distributed throughout the colonies for all to see. Caleb obtained a copy from a tavern in town and brought it back for his family and the Rutledge's to read. It was Sunday and they had all gathered as was their custom for a picnic after church. This time it was Caleb's turn to read the document to everyone. After reading the first part, there appeared to be several questions so he stopped so that each concern could be discussed.

"What does it mean when the document said, 'Laws of Nature and Nature's God?'" Sarah asked.

---

1. Direct quote from the beginning of the Declaration of Independence

"Sarah, we all believe that everything we see was created by Almighty God." John replied. "It is His land, His sky, and all created animals and man owe everything to Him. He also created the laws under which everything operates. Isn't it appropriate that the document acknowledges God early on?"

Caleb added, "Most folks do believe as you say that God created everything as the Bible says:

'In the beginning, God created the heavens and the earth'[2]

Caleb added, "Dad, I know, though, that some folks have an issue with that idea that God did it all. I think they feel it all happened naturally without God."

"That is their right, Caleb, but I do not agree. I have heard some of those arguments, but we forget that none of them can be proven. We cannot go back in time to view how everything began. Do we believe what men say with very limited knowledge especially of past events or do we trust in God and His Bible. Men have tried to destroy the Bible for hundreds, even thousands of years and it is still here while men's ideas have come and gone."

Mary supporting her husband, "I agree with John, and I know that God exists, and that the Bible is true. I have sensed His presence. I have prayed and watched prayers answered. I have felt His presence during difficult times. I know God did it. I think the writers of this Declaration are right and proper to acknowledge God. I think as the Bible says:

'The fear of the Lord is the beginning of wisdom; and the knowledge of the holy is understanding.[3]

---

2. Genesis 1:1

3. Proverbs 9:10

I wonder how many nations and people have been led astray by false teachings. It is good we are building on something tried and true."

"Ok, I get it but what about the idea that all men are created equal?" Sarah interjected and then added with a wry soft giggle: "Does that mean women too?"

Joshua responded, "It means what it says that all of us are created equal, everyone. The use of the term men in the Bible often includes women as well."

Sarah smiled as she looked over at Joshua, she liked that idea.

Elizabeth a bit puzzled, "How about the slaves, we do not seem to treat them as created equal?"

"I think it means them too." Thomas replied, "The Genesis *account says:*

'And God said, let us make man in our image, after our likeness;' and then in the next verse: 'So God created man in his own image, in the image of God created he him; male and female created he them.'"[4]

Mark, Joshua's brother, asked, "Then why do we have slavery?"

"Wow, that is a hard one to explain," Thomas answered, "but the short answer is that it is because of man's sin and the resulting curse of man because of his sin. Mark, when I worked years ago on a plantation, I worked right alongside many slaves. I became friends with a lot of them. I found they were just people trying to make their way in the world just like your mom and me. I even talked with the master of the plantation and found out that secretly he did not believe in slavery either. He was a Christian and could not reconcile slavery with the Bible teachings. He also knew that to just release all the slaves on his plantation would be detrimental to everyone. He needed them to work on the plantation. They

---

4. Genesis 1:26-27

also would have no way to make a living outside of the plantation. Many came to him as adults with little education. Black slaves told him that they had been taken by other stronger, more powerful Black men and sold to the slave traders, which in turn brought them to the colonies and sold them there. The plantation master felt it would be cruel to just set them free. He tried to treat his slaves well, with dignity and for some, that he could educate, teach them a trade, he planned on quietly freeing them."

John asked, "Did you know that of the thirteen colonies, there are twelve that have slaves? The heaviest concentration is in the south where the larger plantations are located. Many of the northern plantations have already freed their slaves. Some leaders that I have talked to even feel that slavery will eventually be abolished in time. It is hard to change opinions."

"I am not sure I understand "created equal'." Mary responded. "Does that mean that everyone is the same and we all should get the same number of things? That seems contrary to how we were all brought up."

"Mary, I do not think that God meant that all of us should have the same amount of wealth and things, Thomas replied, "because to do so would leave the idea of work out of the equation. The Bible says:

'...If any would not work, neither should he eat'[5]

Think of it this way, if a group of men line up at the start of a race, everyone has an equal chance of being the winner at the end. However, after the race starts, not all will cross the finish line at the same time. Usually there is only one ultimate winner, and the rest will be in line behind him. Where they place will depend on their preparation, their effort, the circumstances during the race and so forth. We talk a lot about freedom here in the colonies, but freedom does not mean everyone gets the same

---

5. 2 Thessalonians 3:10

things. It means everyone has the same chance to work and go after their dreams. That is why Elizabeth, and I came here. It was hard. We worked hard. There were setbacks but we kept on going. Now we are seeing some of the fruit of our labor."

"I agree we need to work;" Elisabeth interjected, "some folks like the slaves are at a disadvantage and cannot win the race."

John added, "Elizabeth, you forget one thing; this life is not all there is. The Bible clearly says:

'For God so loved the world that He gave His only begotten Son that whosoever believes in Him shall not perish but has everlasting life.'[6]

Thomas agreed with John, "The race is not over until we die. At that time, God Himself who will reward each person. For those who have ignored God and lived only for themselves; those that have cheated to obtain earthly wealth and goods, those that have done a host of other things against God and His Commandments, will have to face the final judgement seat. The most powerful man, the richest man, will have no advantage over the poorest among us. I even suspect that the poor, rich in faith, may in fact be the real winners of the race! If that is in fact true, it would be better to be born in slavery and must depend on God than to be born in a king's palace without faith."

"Wow," exclaimed Elizabeth, "I had not thought of that. Maybe there will be more slaves in heaven than anyone else."

Caleb asked, "What do you think about this unalienable right of life, liberty and the pursuit of happiness?"

Thomas answered, "I think that based on the first part which says Laws of Nature and Nature's God that it follows that God has given to every

---

6. John 3:16

man the right to life, liberty, and the pursuit of happiness. It is not given by men, a king or a government. It is a gift given by God. It cannot be taken away; it is unalienable."

At that moment, Elizabeth remembered her encounter with the young woman and her lifeless child on the snow. She thought in her mind that this young woman had deprived her child of life, liberty, and the pursuit of happiness. Her anger flared for a moment and then subsided as her compassion returned. She just wished that she had not chosen such a drastic solution to her problem.

Joshua asked, "Caleb, what did it say about governments?"

Caleb: answered, "Governments derive their powers from the consent of the governed."

"Then ultimately governments are supposed to serve the people not the other way around! Is that what I am hearing?" Joshua asked.

"If I understand this," interjected Thomas, "governments are to protect our unalienable rights to life liberty, and the pursuit of happiness and if they fail to do this, it is the right of the people to change or abolish it. So yes, Joshua, I think government is supposed to serve and protect the people against all abuses from the outside or the inside of the nation."

Caleb exclaimed, "That includes abuses from the government as well!"

Everyone said "amen" to that statement.

Caleb added, "The rest of the document summarizes the abuses of Great Brittain and then lists the specifics one by one. I will let you read those for yourself, many of them we can identify with like continually interfering with local governments, keeping a standing army in a time of peace, cutting off trade, taxation without representation, bringing in foreign mercenaries, to name a few. I think the document makes an exceptionally good case for declaring our independence."

The document was passed around for all to look at and talk about. There was more discussion. Eventually they all decided to ponder what they had learned and went home.

Chapter 6

Depression

Both Joshua and Caleb both talked to their parents about joining the Continental Army. Their parents understood their desire and were even proud of the decision. Elizabeth and Mary were, of course, concerned for their safety but they knew that their young men (that is what they were now) needed their support. Joshua wanted to go back to Boston to see Jessica to smooth over and restore their relationship. When he arrived at the store, he could not find her, nor did he see her father. Her uncle was minding the store, and he asked him about her. The uncle told him that she and her father had left on a ship bound for Nova Scotia. Joshua was dejected at the news. He asked the man if he knew when they might return.

Uncle answered, "They may never return."

Joshua asked, "Why did they leave?"

"You know they were loyalists," the uncle replied, "loyal to the King of England, don't you?"

"Well yes but."

Uncle continued, "They knew the Declaration of Independence was coming. When it did, it made every loyalist in the colonies who supported the King traitors to the cause. It was going to be either a fight or flight. They chose flight. They left me with the store because they knew I sympathized with the Patriots and the store might not be destroyed as others have been."

"Did she say anything to you before she left?" Joshua asked.

"No," the uncle answered, "but I knew she was pretty dejected."

Joshua thinking she was still upset with him,

"She was still angry with me."

Uncle sensing Joshua needed some comfort, "Listen lad, I do not think that was it. She was depressed at having to leave you. She told me that she had made you think she was angry with you for telling her that you wanted to join the army. She was about to tell you that she had to leave with her father. She loved both of you and could not choose between you, so she feigned anger. That gave her some time to leave without confronting you. You need to forgive her, lad."

Joshua did forgive her. He even felt a little better. She still loved him. He was sad at not being able to see her.

Uncle admonished him, "You need to leave it in God's hands, lad. If it is meant to be, God will work it out. If not, He will bring someone else into your life."

Joshua then departed and went back home, He and Caleb then prepared to enlist. It was early July 1776.

***

After the British left Boston, Washington surmised that the next target of attack would be New York City. That prize would be a choice base of operations. Washington decided to move his army to New York in early May. He sent word on ahead to begin fortifying Brooklyn where he planned to place his army. Joshua and Caleb joined and followed them to New York. It was no simple task to move the army about two hundred-fifteen miles from Boston to New York. They had to march the whole way. They could move twenty miles in a day at most. More likely a lot less than that, considering the number of supplies, ammunition, and the condition of the paths to be taken. It would take a couple of weeks to move that far, and the men would be tired when they arrived. The British, on the other hand, had it easy by comparison. They would just load their soldiers onto the warships and sail the shorter distance by sea. Traveling at four knots, they could reach the New York harbor in less than half the time needed to move Washington's army. The soldiers, meanwhile, would simply relax on board and would not be exhausted upon arrival. It was an obstacle that Washington continually had to fight against during the entire Revolutionary war.

There were other problems as well. Washington was authorized by Congress to recruit more men but only got maybe two-thirds of what he really needed, about nineteen thousand by the time he reached New York. The British forces under General Howe totaled over thirty thousand. The British troops were seasoned veterans. They knew discipline and how to fight a war. The British had been doing it for years against many enemies including the French. They were expected to be able to load their musket and fire it at the rate of three times in a minute. The muskets were not accurate beyond one hundred yards, so the battle lines were generally set at about one hundred yards. Someone once said that you might as well aim at the moon beyond one hundred fifty yards. A fast runner could cover a hundred yards in less than twenty seconds. It would be slower for a soldier carrying a heavy musket and everything else. The British soldier was trained to reload fast enough to prevent an enemy soldier from covering the distance and overpowering his position.

The British also often fired with bayonets fixed at end of the musket so that after a volley was fired, they might attempt to charge a position and fight hand to hand to overpower the enemy. There were also other tactics like staggering the fire of groups of soldiers to increase the frequency of volleys hurled at the enemy. There were difficulties, too, with the muskets. The sights were not very good to aim it. Black powder was used to fire a point-sixty-nine caliber lead ball and after repeated firing, the musket might foul.

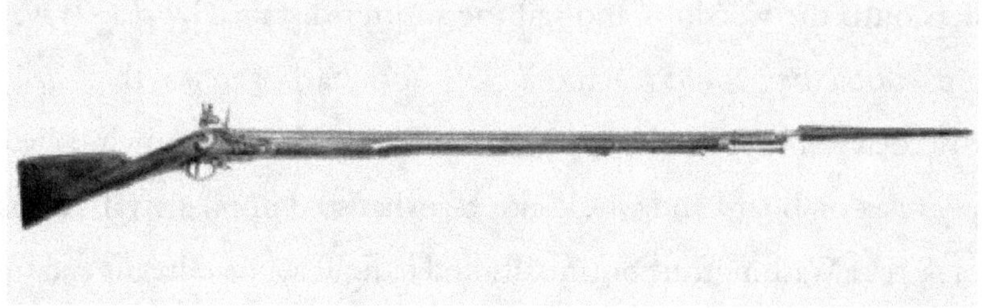

Musket

Both the British and the Americans used the same musket. Washington's army was not well disciplined and trained. Routine orders were not carried out. Muskets were fired in camp when they should not have been fired. Bayonets were used as knives to cut food and making them less useful as bayonets. They also were not on par with the British to reload and fire the muskets. It made them much more vulnerable of being overpowered in a British charge. Nevertheless, Washington was determined to defend New York. He did not want the British to gain control of that valuable port.

The British were preparing too. Two ships sailed up the Hudson River and made it past the American Shore batteries, with the goal of cutting off supplies to Washington's army.

Washington moved the main part of his army to Manhattan but set up fortifications in Brooklyn and on the western end of Long Island.

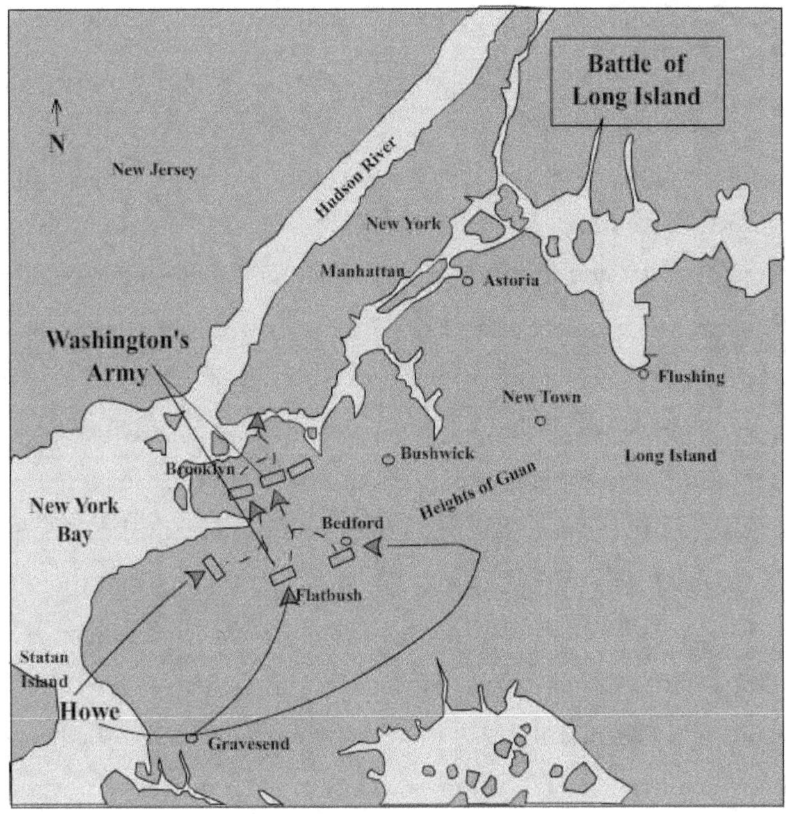

Battle of Long Island

General Howe began landing his troops across the harbor from Long Island on Staten Island in early July. British ships were all over the New York Bay. The population of New York went into a panic at the sight of so many ships. Alarms were set off and American troops rushed to their positions. A week after the initial ships arrived, there were more than one hundred of them in the bay.

Meanwhile news reached Washington that Congress had voted for independence. Washington and several of his brigades marched into the commons of the city to hear the reading of the Declaration of Independence. After the reading, a mob tore down the statue of George III of Great Britain. It was later melted down to make musket balls.

The British General Howe attempted to negotiate through his adjutant with Washington in mid-July, even offering a grant of a pardon. Washington was reported to have said:

"Those who have committed no fault want no pardon." [1]

By mid-August, there were as many as four hundred British ships in New York Bay and reportedly over thirty thousand troops at General Howes disposal. Later five thousand Hessian reinforcements were added. Washington was not sure where the British were going to attack so he split his troops half on Manhattan and half on Long Island. The British decided on a two-pronged attack. A smaller force would attack from the west while a larger force would come at the Americans from the other side at the Guan Heights. The attacks were postponed five days to allow the larger force to move around into position. It did not help the situation that there were many loyalists that welcomed the British and even helped them deceive Washington into thinking that nothing was happening.

Joshua and Caleb found themselves in the front lines on the far westernmost fortification of Washington's army. Their militia was near Stirling's command with five hundred men whom Washington had ordered to defend the westernmost fortifications. General John Sullivan was ordered to use his troops numbering about eighteen hundred to defend the easternmost fortifications. It was about nine AM when the signal was given, and the Hessians began to attack the middle fortification defended by Sullivan. It wasn't long, however, that General Sullivan realized that the main British army was advancing from the rear. All three fortifications were now caught in a two-front attack. Sullivan left his advanced guard to fight off the Hessians while he focused on the British to the rear. Joshua and Caleb managed to fire off a couple of musket balls but soon found

---

1. Wikipedia, Battle of Long Island

themselves in hand-to hand combat with the enemy.

At one point, Caleb was down and about to be bayoneted by a Hessian soldier. Joshua jumped in and bashed the man's head in. The soldier dropped dead at his feet. He had seen death before with animals, but this was the first time he had actually been responsible for the death of another human being. It shocked him and for a moment he could not move. Another Hessian soldier thought to take advantage of the situation, but Caleb killed him before he could hurt Joshua. The fighting was fierce for a brief time and several men on both sides were killed or wounded. Joshua snapped out of his trance and his anger was kindled when he saw another American soldier try to surrender to a Hessian only to be bayonetted by that Hessian. He wanted to kill that soldier on the spot and would have tried except Caleb, seeing that they would soon be surrounded, pulled him away toward the rear fortifications.

Sullivan ordered his men to retreat. Stirling did the same except for a group commanded by Gist that later became known as the Maryland Four Hundred. These men stood their ground even attacking the British and Hessian troops. Most of them lost their lives but did serve as a rear guard to allow the other American soldiers to retreat to safety. Except for the Maryland Four Hundred, it was utter chaos. Washington watched from a nearby hill and was reported to have said:

"Good God, what brave fellows I must this day lose."[2]

The American soldiers had panicked and were running for their lives. In the end, over twenty percent of Washington's forces were either killed, wounded or taken prisoner in the battle. Of those that were taken prisoner, only about half would survive. Howe suffered less than four hundred

---

2. Ibid

casualties killed, wounded, or missing. It was a disaster for the Continental Army and Washington. It could have been even worse. General Howe ordered his troops to break off the attack. The Americans had fled to the fortified rear position at Brooklyn Heights. Howe decided to lay siege to the Americans. From his vantage point, he had the Americans surrounded. He also felt he could control supplies being brought to Washington's army so there was no need to expend more British troops in bloody conflict. He would just wait them out and force them to surrender.

The British began to dig trenches moving slowly closer to the American lines. Howe did not want to duplicate the mistake the British army had done in Boston, by assaulting the American forces in the open. Meanwhile, Washington ordered more troops to be sent from Manhattan to reinforce the beleaguered army. Thomas Mifflin and his Pennsylvania troops responded but upon arrival convinced Washington and the other Generals to evacuate to Manhattan. He and his Pennsylvania volunteers would serve as rear guards. Washington sent word to General William Heath who was at Kings Bridge over the Harlem River to send every available flat-bottomed boat to carry troops across to Manhattan.

At nine PM the troops were told to gather all their ammunition and baggage to prepare for a night attack. Joshua and Caleb gathered their muskets, ammunition and supplies and waited to be told where to take their stand. A few minutes later, officers came around and told the men to be extremely quiet and move out.

Joshua asked, "Where are we going?"

Officer replied, "Don't ask questions. You will see in a few minutes but do NOT make a sound."

Joshua and Caleb obeyed. They noticed as they came upon some wagons and artillery that the wagon wheels had been covered with cloth, apparently to cut down the noise. Joshua wondered where they were going. In about forty-five minutes, he got his answer; they had reached a ferry landing. Flat-bottomed boats were being loaded and one by one left the landing heading across the river to Manhattan. The sick and wounded went first.

Meanwhile, Mifflin's men were tending campfires to deceive the British. The retreat continued through the night. In the morning, Washington was concerned that the evacuation had not gone fast enough, and they would be discovered, but a fog settled in and concealed the movement. By the time the British did realize what had happened, the last man had entered the last boat. Washington had moved nine thousand men across with no loss of life. Joshua and Caleb were glad to be safely in a boat heading away from danger, but they were also sad as were most of the other soldiers. They knew they had lost the battle with the British. The exuberance of pushing the British soldiers out of Boston was now replaced with total dejection. It was not a good time for the army.

Howe gave Washington's Continental army a reprieve for the first part of September but then attacked on September 15th, when he landed a large force into Manhattan. It was a quick defeat of Washington's Continental army. They retreated. The Continental army did surprise the British the following day when the British attacked at Harlem Heights. Washington's army pushed them back. The victory was short lived, as Howe defeated Washington at White Plains. The British were now in complete control of New York City and its harbor, and the city would remain in British hands for the remainder of the war.

Washington withdrew his army across to New Jersey. He needed intelligence as to what was going on in New York. A young man by the name of Nathan Hale volunteered to go into the city and spy for Washington. Unfortunately, he was recognized and turned over to the British by some of his former friends. He was hanged as a spy on September 22nd, 1776. He was twenty-one years old. It was reported that his last words were:

"I only regret that I have but one life to lose for my country." [3]

It became clear that this Revolutionary War would be long and bloody.

Howe now set his sights on two forts up the Hudson River on the north end of Manhattan. They had been built to protect the lower Hudson River against advancing British warships. Howe wanted total control of the Hudson to move his soldiers and cut off supplies to Washington. Fort Washington was the first fort to be attacked on November 16th. It was attacked on three sides: the north, east and south initially and then the fourth when tidal obstacles were overcome. The southern and western sides fell quickly. The Patriots forces fought hard against the Hessian forces on the north side, but they also were overwhelmed. The commander of the fort finally surrendered. The Americans lost fifty-nine killed in action, and over twenty-eight hundred taken prisoner. [4]

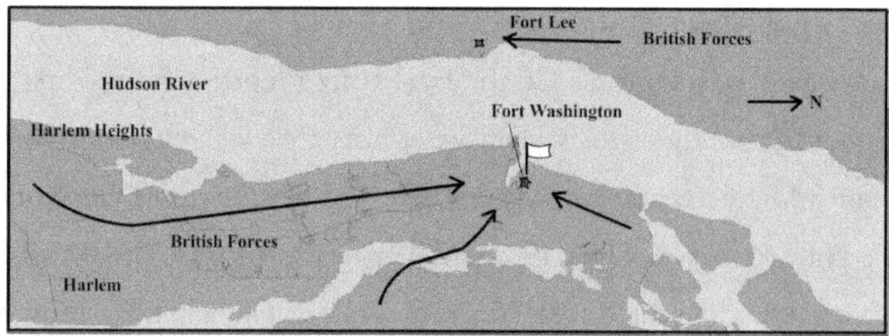

Forts Washington and Lee

The loss was perhaps the worst defeat in the war. It was especially demoralizing to Washington's leaders Henry Knox, Nathanael Greene, William Heath, and Israel Putnam who in June of that year had examined the sight and planned the building of the fort. At the time they felt that, when finished and properly fortified, it would be practically impossible to

---

3. American Battlefield Trust, Nathan Hale

4. American Battlefield Trust, Forts Washington and Lee

take.

Next, General Howe ordered General Charles Cornwallis to capture Fort Lee across the Hudson River from Fort Washington. He attacked on November 20th. The American General Nathanael Greene unable to withstand the attack retreated and abandoned the fort.

The city of New York was now under total British military rule. The loyalists, at first hailed the British triumph, but may have regretted it after a time. Patriot owned businesses were looted and ransacked just like the loyalist business were in Boston. Citizens were hauled in for questioning on almost any pretext. At one point, a fire burned down about one quarter of the city. Some blamed it on Patriots trying to prevent the British from setting up a base of operations in the city. Others said that British soldiers set the fires to justify looting. It was not a good time to be out on the streets.

There was another consequence of a military control, a consequence that was probably as old as armies existed throughout the ages. When the battle is over, soldiers want to drink and have fun. The taverns overflowed with British soldiers. Nathan Hale may well have been caught in one of them. Brothels sprang up almost overnight. There were fights and damage to property almost every evening. The conquerors would take full advantage of the city citizens. It was not something the Loyalists had anticipated.

Washington's army was then pursued across New Jersey, finally taking refuge in Pennsylvania.

Chapter 7

Prescription

Washington's army needed a healthy dose of morale boosting tonic. He found a means with a second pamphlet by Thomas Paine entitled "The American Crisis" published just before Christmas, 1776. He obtained copies and passed them out to his troops while they were camped on the west side of the Delaware River in Pennsylvania. Joshua and Caleb had more book learning than some of the other recruits, so they were elected to read the pamphlet to some of their fellow soldiers. It began:

"These are the times that try men's souls: The summer soldier and the sunshine patriot will, in this crisis, shrink from service of his country, but he that stands it now, deserves the love and thanks of men and woman. Tyranny, like hell, is not easily conquered; yet we have this consolation with us, that the harder the conflict, the more glorious the triumph. What we obtain too cheap, we esteem too lightly; - It is dearness only that gives everything its value. Heaven knows how to set a proper price upon its goods; and it would be strange indeed, if so celestial an article as FREEDOM should not be highly rated. Britain, with an army to enforce her tyranny, has declared, that she has a right (not only to TAX) but 'to BIND as in ALL CASES WHATSOEVER,' and if being bound in that manner is not slavery, then is there not such a thing as slavery upon earth.

Even the expression is impious, for so unlimited a power can belong only to GOD."

Soldier 1, "It sure is a trying time, one to try men's souls."

Soldier 2, "Does he mean that if we succumb to tyranny, we are slaves to that tyranny?"

Caleb replied, "I think so. Our Declaration of Independence says that the government is by consent of the governed."

Joshua added, "Only God who created us has the absolute right to expect us to obey His Commandments. All others earn the right to lead and govern by protecting our right to life, liberty, and the pursuit of happiness. If they try to usurp the roll of God, they should be resisted and even overthrown."

Soldier 1, "Let us hear some more of this."

Joshua read the next paragraph with no interruption. The third paragraph seemed to contain a bit more encouragement. It read:

"I have as little superstition in me as any man living, but my secret opinion has never ever been and still is, that GOD Almighty will not give up a people to military destruction, or leave them unsupportedly to perish, who have so earnestly and so repeatedly sought to avoid the calamities of war by every decent method which wisdom could invent. Neither have I so much of the infidel (unbeliever) in me as to suppose that He has relinquished the government of the world and given us up to the care of devils; and as I do not, I cannot see on what grounds the King of Britain can look up to heaven for help against us: A common murderer, a highwayman (bandit), or a housekeeper has as good a pretense as he."

Soldier 3 emphatically, "Amen!" Joshua read on:

"It is surprising to see how rapidly a panic will sometimes run through a country. All nations and ages have been subject to them.

Britain has trembled like an ague at the report of a French fleet of flatbottomed boats; and in the fourteenth century the whole English army, after ravaging the kingdom of France, was driven back like men petrified with fear; and this brave exploit was performed by a few broken forces collected and headed by a woman. Joan of Arc. Would that heaven inspire some Jersey maid to spirit up her countrymen and save her fair fellow-sufferers from ravage and ravishment!"

The men hung their heads at that last part. They were ashamed of their performance and remembered the story of that brave woman. Joshua read on something about the Tory will "solemnize with curses the day on which Howe arrived upon the Delaware." Paine then summarized the difficulty of defending Fort Lee (he was there) and how they did the best they could to save the troops and as much baggage as they could. He then praised the retreat that the men "bore it with a manly and a martial spirit." Of Washington he said:

"Voltaire has remarked that King William never appeared to full advantage but in difficulties and in action; the same remark may be made on General Washington for the character fits him. There is a natural firmness in some minds which cannot be unlocked by trifles, but which when unlocked, discovers a cabinet of fortitude; and I reckon it among those kinds of public blessings, which we do not immediately see, that God hath blessed him with uninterrupted health and given him a mind that can even flourish upon care (under stress)"

Paine goes on to rail against the Tories even calling the expression of a Tory that said: 'Well give me peace in my day." as unfatherly. He went on to say that

"a generous parent should have said: 'If there must be trouble, let

it be in my day, that my child may have peace"

Soldier 2 asked "Joshua, can you summarize what Paine is saying?"

"Sure." Joshua replied, "He appears to be coming down on the Tories and that they will regret their decision to side with the British tyranny. Many of the Tories are in the south and Paine thinks the war will now come down to them. He says at one point, let me quote:

'I am as confident, as I am that God governs the world, that America will never be happy till she gets clear of foreign dominion. Wars, without ceasing, will break out till that period arrives, and the Continent must in the end be conqueror, for the flame of liberty may sometimes cease to shine, the coal can never expire.'"

Joshua: added, "A little further on he uses an analogy that if a thief should break into his house and destroy it, and even kill his family, and raise the question: should he just allow it? He kind of answers his own question further along in the pamphlet by saying:

'It is the madness of folly to expect mercy from those who have refused to do justice.'"

"He seems to end the essay on an encouraging note," Joshua continued, "by referring to God and that there is no need to fear and that if we persevere, we will be successful. If we are cowardly and submit, our homes will be turned into barracks and bawdy houses for the Hessians."

The pamphlet was then passed around to the men listening for all to examine if they chose. The mood seemed to shift from total gloom and doom from the preceding defeats to one with more hope. Paine did not denounce the retreat; in fact, he praised the discipline and orderliness of it. They began to realize that in war there will be battles lost, perhaps many such battles. It is not the number of battles lost but who is victorious in the end. Now would be the time to face fears, realize the stakes in the war, and bring courage to the forefront. The army now needed a win to cement the new mood.

Washington, knowing his troops needed some encouragement, decided to make a bold move to get back into the fight. On a cold Christmas Eve, 1776, he loaded twenty-four-hundred men into boats and crossed the icy Delaware River. When they reached the other side, the troops marched ten miles in the dark to Trenton, New Jersey. There was a garrison there of some fifteen hundred hated Hessian troops. They surprised the Hessians. A few of them escaped but most were captured, surrendering to Washington. Their commander was mortally wounded in the battle.[1]

1776 had begun on a high note with Thomas Paine's Common-Sense Pamphlet and forcing the British out of Boston. It saw Congress adopt the Declaration of Independence. The months that followed brought defeat after defeat, Battle of Brooklyn, White Plains, Manhattan, Fort Washington, Fort Lee. There had been an execution of a young man, Nathan Hale, by the British. By Christmas Eve, morale was very low. Then came Christmas Day and a Christmas present to Washington's beleaguered army, the capture of the Hessian soldiers. There would be other battles and other losses but at least for now, the army was recovering and beginning to settle in for the long war ahead.

---

1. American Battlefield Trust, Revolutionary War, Trenton

Chapter 8

Better or Worse

After the success at Trenton, New Jersey, Washington decided to push on to Princeton, New Jersey. On January 2, 1777, while the British were sleeping at Trenton, he marched his army around them and on to Princeton. The British forces at Princeton were preparing to move.
1

Joshua and Caleb were at the forefront of the American forces as they came up to Princeton. Suddenly they spotted the British forces, apparently preparing to move out. They were out in the open and did not want to be spotted, so they headed for a nearby orchard. It was too late. Some British soldiers saw them. Soon after the British forces were rushing toward them. Musket balls started flying. One just creased Caleb's head. Both young men thought they were done for when suddenly a rider on horseback galloped toward them at great risk to his own life. It was Washington himself! Right behind him came the American troops. There was another rider as well leading the men. The British saw the Americans, ignored Joshua and Caleb, and concentrated their fire on the American Troops. At one point, after a volley of shots rang out, one of the riders fell from his horse.

---

1. American Battlefield Trust, Revolutionary War, Princeton

Joshua and Caleb thought it was Washington as did the British soldiers. For a moment Joshua and Caleb stood stunned, unable to move. Shortly afterwords, the American forces reached them. They turned and joined in the counterattack on the British. The last part of the battle was fought on Princeton University grounds. The British were routed. Another victory for Washington's army.

Legend has it that at one point in the battle a cannon ball from the Americans decapitated a portrait of King George III. [2] It became a common story that the American soldiers like to tell with a bit of embellishment and mirth. The rider that fell in the battle turned out to be Hugh Mercer, another well-liked General. He was killed, not Washington. Washington and his army then left the area. The sleeping army at Trenton under the British General, Cornwallis, then came to Princeton. He was too late.

He was unable to follow the American army, because Washington ordered the only bridge available to Cornwallis destroyed after he passed over it.

Washington then marched his army to Morristown, New Jersey. There they would spend the winter of 1777.

***

Sybil Ludington of Duchess County, New York was barely sixteen the night of April 26, 1777. She was the oldest of eleven children. Her father was one of Washington's officers in the Continental army. A messenger came by her house to warn her father that British troops were coming.

---

2. Ibid

It was a dark, miserable rainy night and there was no one to warn her father's troops scattered around the countryside. She put her siblings to bed, saddled her horse, and rode off in the dark to warn the troops. The story was that she was able to warn some four hundred of them. She saved them from being surprised by the British. They joined in the battle of Ridgefield. Joshua and Caleb watched later as Washington himself honored her heroism.[3]

On April 27, 1777, the British destroyed supplies stored for Washington in Danbury and then marched on towards Compo beach. At Ridgefield, Connecticut they met about seven hundred patriot fighters who were well armed ready to fight led by Generals David Wooster and Benedict Arnold. The Americans had successfully erected a barricade across the north end of Ridgefield's main street. The Americans held off the British. The town still has a permanent reminder of that battle. The British, as they were leaving, fired off a cannonball that became lodged in a corner post of Keeler Tavern.[4]

3. American Battlefield Trust, Sybil Ludington

In June of that year, the Continental Congress authorized the first official American flag. It consisted of thirteen stripes alternate red and white with thirteen stars in a circle on a field of blue. The legend was that it was designed by Betsy Ross at the request of General Washington. Whether that is true or not is not known.

Not all battles went the way the Continental army wanted. In early July, The British gained the higher ground on Mount Defiance above Fort Ticonderoga. The American commander, realizing he could no longer defend the fort, abandoned it. He and his men narrowly escaped the British soldiers. [5]

The day after the loss of Fort Ticonderoga, some British troops, supported by Loyalists from The King's Royal Regiment of New York and the British Indian Department, ambushed a Patriot militia at Oriskany, New York. The British had been recruiting loyalists to fight against the rebels. They had decided that the best way to fight Americans was with

---

5. American Battlefield Trust, Fort Ticonderoga (1777)

other Americans. The loyalists were victorious. The patriots lost over four-hundred-fifty men killed, wounded, or captured as opposed to only about eighty on the loyalist side. It was a sad time to see Americans fighting Americans. It would not be the last American versus American battle. [6]

The overall British strategy during that summer was to move a contingent of the British army in Canada under the command of General John Burgoyne south to try to divide New England from the rest of the colonies. His movement was slow due to poor roads and many obstacles laid along the route by the Patriots. He also became low on supplies. Upon hearing that there were supplies and horses to be had at Bennington, Vermont. Burgoyne divided his forces and sent some British soldiers along with Loyalists and Indians under Lt. Colonel Frederich Baum, to seize the supplies. American forces led by General John Stark and another regiment under Colonel Seth Warner were waiting for them. Stark was a hero of the Battle of Bunker Hill and Trenton. He knew how to fight the British. It had rained the entire day before the battle. The American militia first attacked with about a thousand men at Walloomsac, New York about ten miles from Bennington during the rain. Baum sent for reinforcements. Loyalist forces came to support Baum. Baum hoped that the weather would slow the American advance until Burgoyne could arrive. When the rain stopped on the morning of August 16th, Stark attacked. He was reported to have said to inspire his me:

"There are your enemies, The Red Coats and the Tories. They are ours, or this night Molly Stark sleeps a widow."[7]

The American forces were able to breach the enemy defenses. It was

---

6. American Battlefield Trust, Oriskany

7. American Battlefield Trust, Bennington

violent. Stark was later reported to have said:

"It was the hottest engagement I have ever witnessed, resembling a continual clap of thunder"[8]

It was a sad battle, however; it was personal. Former friends, who had grown up together in Vermont, were facing each other.

The worse battle that year for the Continental Army was at Brandywine Pennsylvania on September 11, 1777. Washington set up his forces at Brandywine to prevent the British from taking Philadelphia, the seat of the new American government. It was a mistake. He thought he had blocked all the fords across Brandywine Creek. Washington faced Sir William Howe and an army of over fifteen thousand British regulars and Hessian mercenaries. Howe ordered one contingent of his army to attack at the American front at Chadds Ford. Meanwhile under cover of a heavy fog, the major portion of his army crossed the Brandywine further upstream and moved to attack Washington's right flank. Washington's men under command of John Sullivan and William Alexander were on that flank. [9]

Joshua, with Caleb beside him, was located on the right-hand side. As the fog lifted, they saw what appeared to be the whole British army facing them. The attack began. Both young men were barely able to fire off two musket rounds before they were overrun. It was hand to hand combat. Fortunately, both were strong and able to fend off one attacker after another. It soon became clear that there were too many of them. A short time later Joshua and Caleb heard an all too familiar bugle sound calling for a retreat. Soon men were turning and running for the rear. Joshua and Caleb fought off their nearest attackers and did the same. As they neared their

---

8. Ibid

9. American Battlefield Trust, Revolutionary War, Brandywine

lines, there was a cry, and men were setting up to counterattack the British forces.

Washington had ordered a retreat to prevent a total disaster, leaving Nathanael Greene's division to act as a rear guard. Greene's men counterattacked. There was heavy hand to hand combat. When night came, the remaining Americans fell back. It was a crushing defeat allowing the British access to Philadelphia. It was an orderly retreat, however, led in part by a Frenchman, Marquis de Lafayette. The British would now occupy the capital, but the army survived to fight another day.

A little over a week later, while Washington's main army was licking its wounds, Burgoyne's army of over seven thousand soldiers were heading south. The American General, Horatio Gates, with thousands of Americans awaited him at Bemis Heights, just south of Saratoga, New York. The British forces sustained heavy casualties that day and found themselves trapped with a serious shortage of food.[10]

Washington also found his main army needing food and supplies. He also needed to monitor British activity around Philadelphia. There were supplies at Reading. Pennsylvania, so he positioned his army on either side of the Schuylkill River between those two cities. There were other smaller skirmishes, some that did not turn out so well for the Continental army. One of the worst was at Paoli, Pennsylvania. That one was referred to as the Paoli Massacre. About fifty Americans perished in a nighttime surprise attack. Virtually all of them were bayoneted. Patriot propagandists vilified the British tactics. The good battle outcome was at Saratoga. Burgoyne, desperate for a way out of the trap he found himself in, mounted a second attack on October 7. By that time, the American ranks had increased to

---

10. History, American Revolution, The Battle of Bemis Heights

almost double those of Burgoyne. He was pushed back. The British tried to flee but were unsuccessful. They surrendered on October 17th. [11]

The Continental Congress evacuated Philadelphia. Despite losing New York City and now Philadelphia to the British, the battle of Saratoga may well have been the crucial battle that caught the eye of the French. They started to consider that, with a little help, these Americans may well win the war against their hated enemy, Great Britain.

Howe tried one more time in early December to destroy Washington. It amounted to nothing more than a series of small skirmishes. He returned to Philadelphia. Washington and his army headed to Valley Forge for the winter.

---

11. American Battlefield Trust, Revolutionary War, Saratoga

Chapter 9

Interlude

Washington's army marched into Valley Forge on December 19, 1777. It was only about twenty miles from the now British occupied Philadelphia. They were exhausted. They were cold and hungry. Morale was low. They had just lost the capital.

Washington chose Valley Forge because it allowed his army to maintain a defensible position close enough to the enemy to gather intelligence. It also had clean water and firewood. It was lacking in shelter and necessities like food and clothing. It was bitter cold, and diseases took their toll. The conditions were miserable. Even Washington described it as:

"a dreary kind of place and uncomfortably provided."[1]

There were as many as twelve thousand soldiers based there for six months. There were also several women, even children as wives and families joined the men in the camp. Soldiers attempted to build shelters. They had food and blanket shortages. Unsanitary conditions contributed to diseases like smallpox and typhus. There were even shortages of basic clothing like shoes, socks, and coats. Bloody footprints were seen in the snow and ice. The men were exhausted, disheartened, and starving. They

---

1. American Battlefield Trust, Winter at Valley Forge

were volunteers fighting for freedom living in prison camp conditions. As many as three thousand would not be fit for service. Two thousand of them would die just from the camp conditions.

Washington. pleaded with the Continental Congress and the state governors for help. He sent some of his men out on foraging missions to gather supplies from the surrounding countryside. He also had to contend with rivalries among the military leaders. It was an enormous weight on his shoulders. Through it all, his personality, courage, and steady leadership kept the army intact. The men loved and respected their commander. There were no mass desertions nor mutinies at Valley Forge.

Washington appointed Baron Von Steuben to be an unofficial Inspector General of the camp. The men had been in battle but did not have the formal training in discipline, hand-to-hand combat and combat maneuvers like the British troops. Steuben had extensive experience in the seven years' war to prepare him to oversee the military training the men needed. By the time the army left the encampment, the army had been transformed from a ragtag bunch or recruits to a highly disciplined fighting force.

Another addition to Washington's staff was the French officer, Marquis de Lafayette. He endured the hardships right alongside his men and worked directly with them. He was dedicated to Washington and well liked. It may well have been his direct experience with the Continental army and Washington that contributed to convincing the French to ally with The United States on February 6, 1778. [2]

***

---

2. Ibid

The Rutledge's and the Reed's had not heard from either Joshua or Caleb since they had joined the Continental army. They knew that the army had moved south out of Boston toward New York. It made sense that Washington would want to protect and defend probably the next biggest and perhaps the most important port of New York City. The families were desperate for news as to how their sons were doing and war news.

Thomas and John now made regular trips every week into Boston mainly to see if anybody had news. They quickly found out that the best place to find any news at all was the local Green Dragon Tavern near the Commons area in Boston. The tavern was a meeting place both for locals and out-of-towners. The out-of-towners could also obtain lodging. A pint or two of ale soon loosened up the tongue of almost every traveler eagerly willing to tell their tales or others exploits.

Printed documents were also posted on the wooden supports in the tavern. Thomas and John knew that some clergy might not approve of the drinking of beer or ale but, knowing their Bible, they could not quite reconcile that position with the Bible story of Jesus Himself provided wine for the wedding at Cana in Galilee. They became regulars at the tavern and friendly with other regulars. At one time, those patrons included both Loyalists and Patriots and there were a few heated debates between the two groups. After the British troops left Boston, however, there were fewer and fewer Loyalists coming in.

News came weeks or more after the events took place. Couriers on horseback could cover fifty miles or so per day. It would take more time if the roads or weather was bad. The couriers might have to ride through enemy territory and could be captured or killed. Ships could travel with fair wind conditions at about four to seven knots. It was possible to maintain that speed for a full day. People wanting news of events just had to be patient. The first news coming in was disheartening. They heard the Continental army had been defeated at Brooklyn. Later, they heard that Washington and the army had been forced out of Manhattan and then that they were on the run in New Jersey. When they finally heard that the British were now in complete control of New York City, one lone loyalist took the opportunity under the influence of too much ale to rail against the Patriots for their rebellion.

Loyalist shouted, "See, I told you we shouldn't be rebelling against the King. Now you are going to pay for that!"

His outburst nearly got him killed by Patriots in the tavern. Thomas and John happened to be there when it happened, and they successfully intervened.

"Are we not all Americans?" Thomas asked, "We may disagree and are we not fighting for the right to disagree? We should never fight against each other. America has enough enemies in the world."

Fortunately, there were a few other cooler heads in the room. The loyalist was encouraged to leave, and things settled down. The atmosphere was a bit dreary, the next time they gathered, they hoped for some better news. Thomas and John did not like bringing the discouraging news back to Elizabeth and Mary. They knew they would worry even more for their sons.

The news continued to be bad through the fall of 1776. Then winter set in making it harder to get any news. There was a somber atmosphere in the tavern during those days. They did get a copy of Paine's pamphlet "The American Crisis". For some, it may have helped. For Elizabeth and Mary, they needed news that their sons were ok.

It was the better part of a month before the news of Washington's bold move and success at Trenton and then Princeton, New Jersey reached the Tavern. There were cheers and a few hosted toasts at that news. Later, they heard that the army would be wintering in Morristown, New Jersey. Getting news to or from Morristown would be difficult because couriers would have to travel near to enemy positions in New York City. John asked those in the tavern if he might pray for the troops. They nodded yes. John then prayed:

"O Lord God, Father in Heaven, we have been told to pray for our leaders that we might lead peaceable lives. I now ask you to put a hedge of protection around our Continental Government, George Washington, and his army, and those that would help us in our fight for freedom. Please protect them and guide them through these perilous times. We also pray specifically for our sons in the army, that you keep them from harm and bring them back safely to us. We ask these things in the precious name of Jesus, Amen."

The entire tavern answered, "Amen!"

The rest of that year, a trickle of news came in about various battles and skirmishes. Some news was good, like the battle of Ridgefield Connecticut and Bennington, Vermont where Patriots were victorious.

There were losses also, Fort Ticonderoga, the Battle of Oriskany, New York, the loss at Germantown, Pennsylvania, and of course the biggest loss at the Battle of Brandywine, Pennsylvania. The tavern was very silent at that news; they knew that the capital city of Philadelphia had fallen. John was asked to pray again for the troops when they heard that news. When they heard the news of the battle of Paoli, Pennsylvania where some fifty Americans were slaughtered in a brutal British attack, some of the regulars at the tavern made a dummy, dressed it in a British uniform and hung it outside the tavern for all to see.

Then came some good news later that the British surrendered at Saratoga, New York. That news was met with some loud cheers and a few raises glasses. The mood was brighter that day. It was also cold. Winter had set in, and it looked like a bad one. John prayed again for the troops. In fact, it had become a regular occurrence for either Thomas or John to pray for the fledgling nation and the troops.

They heard that Washington and the troops were now wintering at Valley Forge. Someone suggested that maybe they could get letters to their sons at that location. Likely they would be there for the winter, and it looked like it was going to be a long and cold one. Thomas and John, who both wanted to write to Joshua and Caleb, told the others that everyone should come back the following day with their letters. Someone else said that they knew of someone who may be able to get them through to the troops. Some of the wealthier regulars said they would chip in some money for the courier. It was settled. The next weekend the letters were collected and sent out with a prayer that they would make it to the soldiers.

***

It was a very cold February day when Joshua and Caleb both heard their names called out by their immediate commanding officer. They had no idea why until he handed each of them a letter. The young men realized that somehow their families had heard where they were and sent letters to them. The letters in their hands made the day seem just not quite as cold. They brought the letters over near the campfire and out of the wind. Each young man opened his with great anticipation. They devoured each sentence on the pages. In each letter was also a one-pound note (British currency). They knew it had to be hard to get that with money in short supply. The colonists often traded things rather than used actual currency. They appreciated the thought, even though there were no stores close by where they could spend it on things they needed. Joshua and Caleb each read their letters and then read them to each other. There was love, care, and news from home. Every member of the family had something to say to them. Joshua and Caleb knew that their mothers collected each input and put it down on the pages. It was Christmas in February; they had finally gotten their Christmas present.

They searched the camp for some paper and some writing pens. They planned to try to send back letters to their families. They did not know how they could do it but if their families could find a way, then they could too.

As Joshua was writing his letter, he thought about Jessica. He wished he knew where she was and how to reach her. He would write to her if he only knew.

***

In Halifax, Nova Scotia, Jessica was helping her father with some work at a store that he had acquired after arriving there. Perhaps at the same moment that Joshua was thinking of her, her thoughts were filled with him. She remembered his shyness, his handsome features, and how easily he became flustered if she showed just a little annoyance with him. She scolded herself for playing with him like that, but she had to admit it was fun. She smiled as she thought of him and then tears swelled up in her eyes when she realized she did not know where he was. Was he wounded or worst yet, had he been killed in this awful war? She wished she could write to him. How could she do that when she did not know where he was. She pondered it for a while. Then the thought occurred to her that she could write to her uncle back in Boston. Perhaps her uncle could get a letter to his parents. If anyone knew where he was, certainly it would be them.

Jessica knew that her father would not approve of her trying to contact Joshua. She had some heated conversations with him about their relationship.

"Jessica," Her father interjected, "do you not understand that he is a commoner, a farmer. We are merchants and have a different place in society. We live in the city; he lives on a farm. Do you really want to be a farmer's wife? Besides he is a Whig, a rebel against the King. We had to leave Boston because of such people. How is that ever going to work? I will have none of it."

She loved her father, but she loved Joshua as well. She was torn. She wished her mother had lived. She died giving birth to her brother. Her aunt raised her, and she could have confided in her, but she was in Boston. She would have understood, though; her uncle and her aunt were sympathetic to the Patriot cause. There had been a lot of arguments in that household.

Her father was in regular contact with her uncle by ships traveling between Nova Scotia and Boston. She could add her letter to his. She knew her father and that she could persuade him to let her write a letter to her uncle as well. She would then try to persuade her uncle to help her. She carefully considered how she would accomplish it without arousing her father's suspicion. When she had the scheme, all worked out, she smiled.

***

Elizabeth made her way into town to obtain some needed supplies from the dry goods store. When she entered, a man saw her and asked if she was Mrs. Rutledge. She responded yes and he gave her a letter addressed to Mr. and Mrs. Rutledge, Boston Massachusetts. She had no idea who it was from or what it was about. She moved to the side so as not to get in the way of customers and opened the letter. Inside was a note and another letter. Jessica had introduced herself on the note, explained who she was, and how she knew Joshua. She then asked if they knew where Joshua was. If they knew, would it be alright to pass her letter on to him. She explained that she knew she was asking a lot, but she was worried about him and missed him. Jessica had ended the note with a prayer that they were well and would consider her request. Elizabeth smiled at the note. She had seen Jessica a couple of times after she realized her son now had a girlfriend. As mothers often do, they investigate such things. She remembered Jessica as quite a striking young lady. Joshua had good taste, she thought. Without knowing it, Jessica had waited on her once in the store.

Elizabeth had the opportunity to investigate her at close range. Women seem to have an instinct about people. Men can often be oblivious to subtle clues emanating from people, but women are fine tuned to such clues. That is why fallen women can so easily lead men astray. Men do not see the danger. Even with just one meeting, Elizabeth could see that Jessica was a nice girl with good manners, and a good upbringing. She may have been a bit spoiled but basically a caring person. Elizabeth decided that she would try to get Jessica's letter to Joshua. She also went up to the man that gave it to her, found out that he was Jessica's uncle, and asked if she might have Jessica's address so that she could write her back. The uncle said that would be fine and added that he was in regular contact with Jessica's father through merchant shipping and he would be glad to add her letter in the next communication. Elizabeth thanked him. She wrote a short letter introducing herself and later gave it to him.

Sometime later Joshua heard his name called out again. It was another letter. He did not think that his letter had time to reach his parents yet so who could this be from. When he opened it, his eyes got wide, and he grinned from ear to ear.

Caleb: asked, "What are you so happy about in this God-forsaken place?"

"I got a letter!" Joshua exclaimed,

"Oh Oh Ok... So"

Joshua: added, "It's from Jessica! Somehow, she has found me!"

The rest of the day, Caleb was not able to wipe the smile off his face even though the temperature was well below zero.

***

The mood at Valley Forge was somber at best. The men had left their homes and family and volunteered for this fight. After Boston, they thought they had a chance to win. They were not so sure now. They had lost New York city and now the capital city Philadelphia. They had seen many of their fellow soldiers killed or wounded. Many others had left the ranks to return home. Those that did, had farms and their families to tend to. They had only volunteered for a short duration. It was now clear that this war would be long and painful. It also pained them when they thought about it, that so many of their former friends and even some relatives were fighting against them as Loyalists on the British side. Did they not realize that the atrocities of the British Parliament and King George III, which they all felt, were the very reason the Continental army was fighting this war? The soldiers felt angry at being betrayed, after all they were fighting for freedom for everyone including the Loyalists.

Johua and Caleb befriended many of the soldiers while at Valley Forge.

They almost had to; they were all in this together and sometimes had to share things, even a cup for coffee because things were in short supply. They trusted Washington, that he knew what they needed and would do his best to get those things for them. They just needed to have faith. Joshua and Caleb met several black men in the camp and began talking with them. There were some black men in the army and those that were, fought well side by side with the other soldiers. Joshua's father told them many times of befriending black folks while working on the plantation as an indentured servant and that he found them just people like himself, just trying to live and survive this life. As a result, Joshua and Caleb did not harbor any animosity toward black folks.

At one point, they talked with one man named Samual. Samual was quiet at first but, as time went on and he got to know Joshua and Caleb better, he began to talk to them. Samuel told them that he had been a slave on a plantation in Virginia before the war. After the war started and the Patriots made an offer to reward any slave who would fight for the rebellion their freedom when it was all over. The British had done the same thing, but it did not mean the same thing.

Samual, "They gave me a musket and offered me freedom."

Joshua asked, "Samual, what did freedom mean to you?"

Samual thought about it and replied, "At the beginning, I did not know what it meant. I only knew that I did not want to be on the plantation no more."

Joshua probed, "So you signed up."

"Yep"

"Do you have a better understanding of what freedom means now?" asked Caleb.

"Some," Samual replied, "but I am still pondering it."

"I can understand that; I am too." added Joshua.

Samual surprised, "You? How can that be, you was born free?"

"Samual, I think we are all under some kind of bondage." Joshua explained, "My father and mother worked on a plantation too and were bound by the agreement to work hard for five years. After that they were given a piece of land, some fifty acres, which they could now farm. Once they had the land, the land was their master demanding a whole lot of hard work to clear it, plant it, work it, and build on it. When they had children, I am their oldest, the children demanded their time. The need for food, clothing, and other necessities demanded their attention. My parents were never free to just walk away and do whatever they wished."

Samual furrowed his brow, "I never thought about it like that."

Joshua continued, "The Bible speaks of bondage, kind of like slavery. Even the children of Israel were in bondage (slavery) for four hundred years. There are other passages like 'the borrower is servant to the lender.' In that sense, my parents were in bondage to the plantation owner until the debt for the land was paid. Samual, do you know the Bible?"

Samual replied, "Yes, I do. We all went to church on Sunday. That was the best day of the week."

Joshua probed further, "Samual, do you know the Lord? I mean personally, have you accepted Jesus Christ as your Savior?"

"I know about Jesus." Samual replied.

Joshua attempting to clarify, "Samual, The Bible says that the devil also knows about Jesus and trembles. He is not, however, going to go to heaven and he knows it!"

Samual puzzled, "What must I do, then." Joshua replied, "The Bible says:

'For all have sinned and come short of the glory of God. [3]

'The wages of sin is death; but the gift of God is eternal life through Jesus Christ our Lord. [4]

Joshua added, "But then in another passage it says:

'But God commendeth his love toward us in that, while we were yet sinners, Christ died for us. [5]

Joshua continued taking note of Samual's countenance that he was following, "Then in John it says:

'For God so loved the world that he gave his only begotten Son that whosoever believeth in him should not perish but have everlasting life. [6]

"Does this make sense to you, Samual?" Joshua asked.

"Yes sir."

Joshua added, "Would you like to receive this gift of eternal life?"

"Yes."

Joshua looked Samual in the eye, "If this makes sense, then I can lead in a prayer, and we can tell it to God. Would you let me do that?"

Samual with eyes wide, "Yes sir."

Joshua bowed his head and led in a simple prayer something like:

"Lord, I know I am a sinner. I know that for my sins I deserve death and hell. I understand that Jesus died to pay for my sins. The best I know how I am putting my trust in Jesus. Thank you for saving me."

---

3. Romans 3:23

4. Romans 6:23

5. Romans 5:8

6. John 3:16

Joshua knew that Samual prayed that prayer because he recited it word for word as Joshua prayed it.

Caleb had been praying silently as Joshua spoke not wanting to interfere. Unbeknown to them, another black man had been listening quietly to their conversation. He was an older man. When Joshua finished praying with Samual, he spoke up catching Joshua and Caleb by surprise.

Black man interjected, "What do you boys know about bondage?"

Joshua responded, "I was just showing, Samual, that we are all under some kind of bondage."

Black man sternly, "It ain't the same Joshua. Your parents bound were by an agreement and us as property of another man as slaves."

Joshua bowed his head, "I guess your right; I cannot fathom that kind of experience."

Black man emphatically, "No you can't."

His voice was stern as he looked steadily into Joshua's eyes. He seemed to be able to look deep into Joshua's soul. After a time, he softened his stare, realizing that Joshua and Caleb were just trying to be friendly and did not mean any disrespect. Joshua and Caleb both sensed that they were about to receive some wisdom from an older man who had seen things, been through things, and somehow God had given him wisdom.

Black man asked, "You boys want to teach me some more or do you want to listen a while?"

Both responded, "We want to listen."

Black man continued, "My name is Abraham. I was taken many years ago from Africa as a boy. My parents were killed there. I was beaten and marched to the sea, put on a slave ship, beaten some more, brought over here and sold to a plantation owner in Virginia. I grew up working in the fields from sunup to sundown during the spring through to the fall. We worked six days a week and then allowed to rest on Sunday and go to church if we wanted to. At first, I did not want to. I was angry. I rebelled; I was beaten some more. I tried to run away; some other white folks caught me, beat me so bad, that I almost died, and brought me back. I was ready to die."

"I am sorry you were treated that way." Caleb offered.

Abraham added, "I stayed angry a long time. One day there was a man and his wife, came to me after another beating by a field boss. They brought me some food and put some salve to my wounds, and they talked to me. I did not want to listen, but I did not want to be beaten anymore either. The salve felt good. The food tasted good. They gave me some clothes and a blanket and told me to rest. They would make sure no one would bother me while my back healed. They came every day, bringing more salve and more food. One day they brought me a Bible and gave it to me. I told them, it wasn't any use 'cause I did not know how to read. They told me that they would teach me. They did. It took a while, but they were patient and over time I got to reading pretty good. They showed me the same verses that you just quoted to Samual. They asked me if I wanted to pray to receive Jesus. I made excuses and for a long time, I would not! Then one day while working in the field, the field boss did not like what I said to him and was about to give me another beating. As the whip was about to come down on me, the man that had helped me stepped in and the whip hit him instead of me. That field boss suddenly turned white."

Field Boss apologized, "I am sorry master; I did not realize it was you. I am sorry, please forgive me, I I.."

Abraham continued, "I suddenly realized that the man and his wife that had brought the salve, food, and helped me were the plantation owners. They were the masters of plantation. I was their slave!"

Joshua, Caleb, and even Samual listened intently to the story.

Abraham added, "I had not seen him in the fields before. The master was watching me, concerned for me, and when he saw that I was in trouble again, he stepped in. The story of Jesus flashed through my head. I suddenly realized Jesus was the master of the universe! He stepped in to take the punishment for my sin, my anger, my rebellion. Just like the plantation master took the pain of the whip. Tears flooded my eyes. The plantation master saw me and asked if I was now ready to receive Jesus. I said yes. He prayed with me just like you boys just prayed with Samual."

Abraham paused and looked at Joshua and Caleb for a moment. He seemed to be looking into their hearts to see if his words were getting through. After a moment satisfied that they were he continued:

"I have lived many more years than all of you. I have seen good, and I have seen evil. I have thought evil, and I have thought good. I know that my real home is in heaven and in this life, I am just a passing through. I have seen hatred, white folks against black folks and black folks against white. I have learned that not all white folks are bad and that not all black folks are good. It was black folks that first beat me, killed my parents and put me into slavery. It was while folks that cared for me and led me to a saving knowledge of Jesus Christ so that I could be in paradise forevermore."

He paused to let that sink in.

Abraham: added, "The fact is that none of us is good; that is what the Bible says. We have all done wrong and we do well to deal with our own sin rather than constantly pointing out the sin of others. This war is terrible. You and I have seen former friends, maybe even relatives now belittling and fighting each other. Yet we are all Americans! If we had all come together as one, this war would have been over in a short time. We had all the advantage. It was our land. The British had to travel a long-distance taking weeks even months to reinforce their troops. We are all Americans. It isn't right that we are fighting each other. When we stop doing that and live as one people, there will not be a better nation on earth or one that another nation would dare attack."

"Joshua," Abraham looked directly into Joshua's eyes, "you asked Samual earlier what did freedom mean to him? I ask you what it means to you?"

Joshua did not have an answer.

Abraham answered for him, "I believe that freedom is the right to choose who your eternal master is going to be, Jesus or Satan. We all will eventually be bound to one or the other. The Bible contains the truth, and it says the truth shall make you free.[7] "

Samual (thought for a moment): "I think I just got a taste of freedom!"

Abraham: "Yes sir, you did!"

Joshua responded as though a light had been turned on in him, "I think this war is about the freedom to choose who you will serve while you are here."

Abraham smiled.

---

7. John 8:32

Chapter 10

Changes

Both sides made changes in 1778. The British General Howe was replaced by Henry Clinton. The British then turned their sights on the south particularly Charleston, South Carolina and Savannah, Georgia. They felt that if they could secure those ports and maintain control of the port of New York, they could completely control the seas. From those ports they may be able to cut off the supplies from reaching the American army and perhaps force Washington into submission and surrender. Washington had been a thorn at times to the British and they relished the thought of making him bow to the British crown.

There were changes on the American side as well. Von Steuben had succeeded in building up the military prowess of the Continental army. The addition of the Marquis de Lafayette added a very capable leader to Washington's staff. In early February, although it took a while for news to reach the continent, France allied with the United States. That added a naval presence comparable to Great Britain for the American cause.

Battles began again after the long hard winter. The British tried to trap Marquis de Lafayette and his men at Barran Hill, Pennsylvania in May, but he and his men escaped.

The British abandoned Philadelphia In mid-June. Citizens of that city were strongly supportive of the Patriots and there were very few Loyalists. Militias would harass the British from the surrounding small towns whenever the British were on the move outside of the city. It became untenable for the British to maintain occupation of the city. There were many welcome cheers from Taverns throughout the colonies when they received the news.

There was another development after the Continental army moved back into Philadelphia. One of Washington's commanders, Benedict Arnold, met and married Peggy Shippen, the daughter of a prominent loyalist. She convinced her new husband to commit treason and supply intelligence to the British. He was later discovered and had to leave or be executed. He went to England. His former countrymen despised him, and his status in England was not all that much better. He could have died a hero but instead Ben Franklin was said to have described him as a "Judas."

There were some fireworks at the Battle of Monmouth, New Jersey and not just from the muskets and cannons on the field. The Continental army was outnumbered two to one. Washington's commander, Charles Lee, led the initial attack, but he lacked confidence in the ability of the soldiers under his command, so he backed off against the British General Charles Lord Cornwallis. It was a potential disaster. The army was essentially leaderless and started to panic.

When Washington saw what had happened, he galloped to Lee, confronted him in a loud angry retort and removed him on the spot from command. He then rallied the troops. His action led the rest of the Continental army into the battle. Washington then ordered Nathanael Greene's division on the right, General William Alexander's troops on the left and turned over Lee's men to the Marquis de Lafayette and General Anthony Wayne. The British redcoats fell back. The fighting was back and forth under the hot June sun, but by about 6 PM the British had enough. They did not give Washington another chance the next day; they slipped away in the night. [1]

In July, it was reported that George Rogers Clark captured Kaskaskia, in what became known as Illinois. The British apparently were taken by surprise and Clark accomplished the capture without firing a shot.

The first combined French and American battle engagement was the besiege of Newport, Rhode Island. The French assisted but weather spoiled plans on both sides. Eventually after a month of siege, the American commander Sullivan, put up such a strong resistance that the British decided to leave. [2]

***

New York was under firm British control throughout all the battles, but the citizens of New York suffered under the military rule in the city. The loyalists may not have felt quite as happy with their choice of sides as well. They suffered too. Many were conscripted to fight in with the British. They had been and were now not just disagreeing with their fellow Americans but were enemies of those Americans. Loyalists in all the towns around New York, where the Continental army was victorious or where Patriot leanings were strong decided to leave those towns and go to New York. The New York City population swelled. It became even more difficult for New Yorkers.

---

1. American Battlefield Trust, Revolutionary War, Monmouth

2. American Battlefield Trust, Revolutionary War, Rhode Island

***

The opening move in the British southern strategy began at the very end of December 1778. It was the first battle of Savannah, Georgia. It pitted the local Patriot militia and the Continental army against a British force under the command of Lieutenant Colonel Archibald Campbell. There was a strong loyalist sentiment there and that may have helped the British achieve the win. The British hoped that by gaining Savannah they could subdue more of the rebellious south. [3]

Unlike the northern winters, southern winters were relatively mild, and battles could still be fought. In early February, one such battle was fought near Beauford, South Carolina also known as the battle of Port Royal Island. It pitted Major General William Gardiner's British forces against the forces of Brigadier General William Moultrie. Among Moultrie's men were a few African Americans, a militia unit recruited from Charleston's Jewish population and two signers of the Declaration of Independence, Thomas Heyward, Jr. and Edward Rutledge. Both sides exchanged fire and slugged it out. Eventually Gardiner broke off the fight.[4]

There were other small battles in February like the Battle of Kettle Creek, Georgia in which the Patriots decisively defeated loyalist militia forces. [5] George Rogers Clark captured Vincennes in what became later known as

---

3. Wikipedia, Capture of Savannah

4. Port Royal Island Battle Facts and Summary | American Battlefield Trust (battlefields.org)

5. American Battlefield Trust, Revolutionary War, Kettle Creek

Indiana. [6] There were losses too like the one at Brier Creek in early March. They suffered significant losses there and morale also suffered. [7]

War is hell. It brings out both the best in men and the absolute worst. Men become heroes when they stand their ground and fight without any concern for their own safety or charge out to rescue their fallen comrades. They are regarded often with horror at some actions when they appear to go on a rampage of wonton killing. Their actions may in both cases represent two sides of the same coin. To be brave in battle often means that you also must be oblivious to the blood and gore of battle. Some feel that the best soldier is one that will hate the enemy. If he has compassion in the heat of battle, he may not fire his weapon and some of his fellow soldiers may die as a result.

Bad things did happen on both sides. The British and Hessians were accused of bayonetting soldiers after they had surrendered. The American side also had incidents that they would not be proud of. In June of 1779, for example, there was a military campaign against four Native American tribes that had allied with the British. Washington had ordered the campaign in retaliation for the loyalist and Indian attacks on Wyoming Valley, German Flatts, and Cherry Valley and later Fort Freeland, PA, where British and Indians attacked the fort mostly comprised of women, children and old men. The British and Indians were attacking settlers in the western regions not soldiers. Washington was angry. Sullivan may have carried the retaliation too far. The goal had been to bring the war home to the enemy to break morale. The campaign attacked forty villages, destroyed crops and stores and chased some five thousand Iroquois to Fort Niagara

---

6. American Battlefield Trust, Revolutionary War, Vincennes

7. American Battlefield Trust, Revolutionary War, Brier Creek

for British protection. The area was depopulated. Some have described the expedition as genocide. [8]

In June 1779, Spain declared war on Great Britain. Spain's king was not willing to directly align with the United States. It would not be good for one imperial power to the colonies to encourage another to revolt. It could backfire. He was persuaded, however, to align with the French against Great Britain. An ally of an ally to the United States in fact then became an ally of the United States. [9] The British started the war against just one nation, now she would be fighting two.

A few weeks later, about two thousand British soldiers landed at Fairfield, Connecticut which had supported the Patriot cause for independence. The soldiers sought to punish the town by burning it down.

Americans captured Stony Point, NY, located thirty miles north of New York on the Hudson River in July. It was not really a true fort but had a favorable position on the river. American General Wayne attacked but Washington was also very much involved. He ordered the men to advance with unloaded muskets and bayonets so as not to alert sentries. He also ordered the men to pin pieces of white paper to their hats so they could identify friend from foe. By the time the British detected the attack, their artillery was useless; it could not be angled at the invaders. The British were quickly overwhelmed. [10]

There were other battles. The Americans and the French tried un-

---

8. Wikipedia Sullivan Expedition

9. History, This Day in History, June 21 Spain Declares War against Great Britain

10. American Battlefield Trust, Revolutionary War, Stony Point

successfully to retake Savannah. There was also a naval battle. John Paul Jones, a seasoned sailor who had joined the Continental navy in 1775, now the captain of the Bonhomme Richard, engaged the HMS Serapis and a smaller Countess of Scarborough, who were escorting a merchant fleet. The British ships inflicted considerable damage to the Bonhomme Richard, and the captain asked Jones if he had struck his colors indicating surrender. Jones replied from his disabled ship:

"I have not yet begun to fight."

They fought on for three more hours. The Serapis and The Countess of Scarborough surrendered. The Americans transferred to the Serapis and the Bonhomme Richard sank the next day. [11]

---

11. History, This Day in History September 23

Chapter 11

Hardship

In November of 1779, Washington and his army went back to Morristown, New Jersey for winter. They would be there six months. Valley Forge had been hard, but Morristown turned out to be even worse. There was an intense cold, the coldest on record that winter. How cold was it?

One officer commented, "Those who have only been in Valley Forge or Middlebrook during the last two winters, but have not tasted the cruelties of this one, know not what it is to suffer."[1]

Another said, "The passage of the North [Hudson] River, even in its widest part...was about the 19th [of February] practicable for the heaviest cannon, an event unknown in the memory of man."[2]

The army cut down trees from the surrounding countryside and used them to build log cabins for shelter. They had to dig into the frozen ground first to lay the first logs to prevent the freezing wind and snow from penetrating the cabins. Each cabin was designed to house twelve men. The area became a log cabin city housing ten to twelve thousand men. There were

---

1. Attributed to *Major General John Kalb*

2. *New York: British Major General Pattison to Lord George Germain in London, February 22, 1780*

desertions, disease, deaths, shortages of food and supplies. Shoes, shirts, and blankets were in short supply. It was said that some soldiers ate tree bark to satisfy their intense hunger. The first line in Paine's "The American Crisis" was lived out in Morristown.

"These are the times that try men's souls."

Washington was extremely frustrated. It was the responsibility of each state to supply the needs of the army. He was forced to seek food from the surrounding farms. Drought, however, had created shortages in the harvest season. Farmers also cut back on the amount of land they cultivated because of the very poor prices offered by the Continental army. Civilians were extremely reluctant to accept the Continental paper money. They felt it was almost worthless. If they did accept it, they had to raise the price for anything they sold incredibly high in hopes that it would be worth something later.

"The times are growing worse from hour to hour." A third officer added, "The dearth of necessaries of life is almost incredible and increases from day to day. A hat costs four hundred dollars, a pair of boots the same, and everything else in proportion. The other day I was disposed to buy a pretty good horse. A price was asked which my pay for ten years would not have covered. Of course, I did not take it and shall try to get along with my other horses. Money scatters like chaff before the wind, and expenses almost double from one day to the next, while income, of course, remains stationary."[3]

In addition to all of that, the soldiers had not been paid for months. That also meant that their back pay, if they ever received it would be nearly

---

3. *Major General Johann De Kalb from undated letter taken from "Life of John Kalb" by Friedrich Kapp, c. 1870*

worthless! Not only were conditions terrible, but the fledgling new nation was in ruins financially.

In the spring, regiments from the Connecticut line tried to mutiny. It was quickly put down. Morale was low. In spite of everything, the army persevered, determined to overcome the challenges. Some good news came to Washington in the spring. The Marquis de Lafayette, who had gone back to France, came back with the news that France would send a second fleet of ships to aid the American cause. [4]

---

4. American Battlefield Trust, Washington's Encampment at Morristown, New Jersey and the "hard Winter" of 1779-1780

Chapter 12

Home

Both Joshua and Caleb became sick that winter. Many soldiers died. It was a long hard recovery. When the weather grew a little warmer, they approached their superiors that they might take a leave and perhaps make their way home. The request was not unusual. They had a good reputation, so the request was granted. The officers helped them map out a route that would have them bypass the area around New York City to avoid any British soldiers. It would mean that they had to cross the Hudson River well upstream. It would add distance to their journey, and it would take longer but would be safer. They left the camp.

***

They had to work their way considerably up the Hudson River above New York before they found an area where the river narrowed enough to make it possible to cross. At that point they were extremely fortunate. They found some Patriot sympathizers with boats willing to take them across. When the men realized they were soldiers in Washinton's army, they took Joshua and Caleb across for free and even gave them some supplies for their trip. The young men felt that God was looking out for them.

Once across the sympathizers mapped out a path for them to follow and they made their way eastward. The roads were not used much that far north so the going was a little slower but also safer. The British did not go that way either. Part way across the state, they met some farmers on the road. The farmers introduced themselves as Patrick Smith and Robert Harris. They had a wagon and invited the young men to ride with them. After a while Patrick and Robert realized they were soldiers in Washington's army. They also had sons in the army and asked if Joshua and Caleb knew them. They did not, but then it was hard to know everyone. They understood and talked for an hour or so. They told Joshua and Caleb that they had gone to a town to get some seed for planting and that is what was in the bags that were beside them. They talked about their families. They asked many questions about how the fighting was going and the condition of the troops. Then they were silent for a bit as they approached one of the farms.

Patrick whispered to Robert, "We need to help these boys."

"How?" replied Robert.

Leaning closer to Robert so the young men would not hear, "Well, we both have an extra horse that are a bit older but still good. I think we ought to give these boys the horses and help them get home. What do you think?"

Robert thought about it, "I think you are right. We need to do our part. I hope if our boys try to come home, someone will help them too. "

"Then you agree?" Patrick whispered.

"Yes."

Patrick looked back at Joshua and Caleb and told them what they planned to do.

Joshua protested, "We do not have money to give you for the horses."

"That is OK, boys." Patrick responded, "It's a gift. It is kind of like we are giving the horses to our own sons; kind of paying it forward in the hope that someone will be kind to our own boys."

Robert added, "You take the horses and welcome."

The farmers gave them the horses, some older but still good saddles along with supplies and sent them on their way. Joshua thanked God for His providence and of course Patrick and Robert.

It took them about ten days to finally reach the outskirts of Boston. When they came upon the old familiar landscape, their hearts began to beat a bit faster in anticipation of seeing home and family. They came upon Caleb's family farm first. Sarah was the first to see and recognize them.

Sarah shouted when she saw them, "It's Joshua and Caleb!"

When they heard her, they all came running. Sarah hugged her brother. She then came over to Joshua. Joshua recalled how he felt the last time he had seen her. He had noticed then that she was beginning to transition to a woman, but now the transformation was complete. He thought she was beautiful, even though her hair was not all fixed in place like Jessica's would have been and her apron was dirty from the work that she had been doing. She hugged him, a longer hug than she had given her brother. She then moved back but put her hand on his arm like she had done the last time he had seen her. It felt... good.... Comfortable. He did not completely understand it. There were some people even women who touched him like Sarah, but when they did it was annoying. Her touch was warm, gentle, pleasant. He liked it.

"Joshua," Sarah said as she came closer to him, "I am so glad to see you home safe. We all were worried about the both of you."

"It is good to be home." Replied Joshua.

"We need to celebrate." Sarah announced, "I know you want to see your parents, but perhaps we can get together after church tomorrow. (They had arrived home on Saturday). You both can tell us all about your exploits and how things are going. Sometimes it is hard to get news about things."

After greeting the others in Caleb's family, Joshua bid goodbye and went on his way toward home.

Thomas was still out in the field when Joshua arrived, so it was Elizabeth who saw him coming first. She almost fainted but quickly recovered herself. She called out for her other children and then sent one of them to go get their father. Joshua came riding up. She could not wait to embrace her son as he climbed off the horse. She held him so tight that Joshua thought for a moment that she would never let him go. A few moments later she did. Then she kissed him and stepped back to look at him. She saw that he had lost some weight. He looked a little pale to her. She touched his face; he realized his mother knew that things had not been exactly good for him. Moms have a kind of instinct for such things.

Joshua seeing his mother's concern, "I have been sick, mom. Caleb too. We are better now, but I could use some of your good home cooking."

He smiled at her, and she felt a little better, but she was curious as to what had happened to them. She would get it out of him later, but for now she was just overjoyed at having him home. Thomas came in from the field a little later, gave his son a hug, and they all went into the house.

"Caleb is with me," Joshua added, "and we stopped by his house first. Sarah suggested that we all get together tomorrow after church and maybe we could talk."

Elizabeth thought, "Sarah suggested????"

She knew her son. She wondered what was going on there with him and Sarah.

The next day they all went to church. Pastor Josiah quickly spotted Joshua and Caleb as they entered the church. They were just about to begin the Hymn "A mighty Fortress Is Our God" written by Martin Luthur of the Protestant Revolution fame. They all sang the first two choruses:

"A mighty fortress is our God, a bulwark never failing,
Our helper He, amid the flood, of mortal ills prevailing.
For still our ancient foe, doth seek to work us woe.
His craft and power are great, and, armed with cruel hate,
On earth is not his equal.

Did we in our own strength confide, our striving would be
losing.
Were not the right Man on our side, the Man of God's own
choosing
Dost ask who that may be? Christ Jesus. it is He
Lord Sabaoth, His Name, from age to age the same. And He
must win the battle."

Joshua thought the hymn was appropriate for the times they were all in. After the hymn, Pastor Josiah encouraged everyone to greet each other.

"Joshua and Caleb, they are our returning heroes."

The young men felt a little embarrassed at being put on a pedestal but accepted the greetings. Pastor went on with his message on "Overcoming with Jesus". Everyone shook their hands as they left the church. Then the Rutledge and the Reed family gathered to see where they might meet. It was April and still a little cooler but not nearly as cold as the winter had been. They decided to go to the Reed farm, which was closest, and gathered in the house with a warm fire in the fireplace.

Joshua and Caleb were given seats of honor in the center so everyone could hear all that they had to say. Sarah carefully positioned herself on a stool next to Joshua, a fact that was not lost on his mother Elizabeth. Hannah, Joshua's sister followed Sarah's example and positioned herself next to Caleb. She was nearly eighteen. Caleb had not seen her for almost four years. He took notice that she had changed. It was a good change. She looked up at him and smiled. He was a little taken with her and smiled back.

All the children started asking one question after another in rapid succession.

"Whoa!, whoa!" Caleb said emphatically with his hands up, "One at a time and let us answer it before you ask another."

They quieted down some and began to ask what was on their mind. Some were about where they had been, how hard it was, what it was like in camp, did you see Washington, and so forth. Some were harder to answer like: "Did you kill some redcoats?"

For most of it, Sarah was quiet but intensely listening. Occasionally she would put her hand on Joshua's arm. Each time she did, Joshua felt a surge of warmth and he liked the feeling. Elizabeth, her maternal senses aroused, noted each time she did it and Joshua's reaction. She wondered how Jessica played into all of this. Had the two of them broken off their relationship? Mary also noticed her son and Hannah. Elizabeth and Mary looked at each other and raised their eyebrows a little as if to say: "I wonder what is going on with them?" Their subtle facial expressions each told the other all they wanted to know, at least for now.

Joshua and Caleb tried to answer all the questions that they felt they could. They did not like to dwell on the bloody parts. Joshua still remembered his first killing of an enemy soldier. He had been brought up and taught the Bible command "Thou shalt not kill." Both young men were having some trouble reconciling that command with what they had done and seen others do in the war. They also knew that the Bible spoke of wars and even God commanding the children of Israel to go in and destroy nations. They were committed to the Patriot cause. Juggling what they knew to be right and how men act could be overwhelming. They knew they should love and not hate their enemies, but when they heard of the senseless killing of surrendering soldiers or the massacre of others, even women and children, their anger was aroused. Even as they thought about it, they could feel that anger. They pushed those thoughts out of their mind. They needed to trust God that He would work it all out and replace those thoughts with happy ones. They were home. They were Ok. They were among those who loved them. Sarah, seeing that Joshua was deep in thought, put her hand on his arm. Hannah did the same for Caleb.

Both young men needed to rest and recuperate. They went to their separate homes and began to help on the farms. Spring was now here, and it was time to prepare the fields and plant. Joshua and Caleb threw themselves into the work. With each passing day, they felt stronger. The war was pushed back in their minds. They began to gain back some weight. Both Elizabeth and Mary were a little concerned with how emaciated they looked when they first returned, but after a while they filled out again. They felt better. There were many more Sundays on which the two families got together after church. They would just alternate the gathering place. When the weather got better, the church congregation would hold a potluck social. Sometimes, there would even be a dance scheduled. Both the ladies and the men would dress up for such events. Joshua and Caleb completely forgot about the war for several hours as they danced with the ladies. Sarah and Hannah made sure they monopolized the dances with Joshua and Caleb.

The time came when the young men felt guilty that they were not doing their part for the war effort. The news had not been all that encouraging. News had finally reached them that Charleston, South Carolina, had fallen to the British and the loyalists. The Patriot forces in Charleston had been under siege for weeks. They eventually ran out of food and supplies were low. The Patriot commanding officer was told by the enemy that he must surrender unconditionally. When he refused, the British bombarded Charleston with heated shot that set the city on fire. The Americans were forced to capitulate. More than five thousand American troops were taken prisoner. [1] It was a terrible defeat, perhaps the worst in the Revolutionary War.

Joshua and Caleb decided they needed to rejoin the army. This time they felt they needed to join Greene's men in the south. They talked it over with their families. Of course, they did not want them to again be in harm's way, but they also knew how the young men felt. Traveling around New York City seemed like a dangerous route to take with the British and loyalist forces completely in control of that city. John, Caleb's father, came up with a viable solution. He had worked on the docks in Boston, and Boston was under Patriot control. British ships still patrolled along the coast, but smugglers had eluded them for years. The new American navy had even managed to defeat some of the heavily armed British warships by luring them into shallow waters causing them to run aground. Joshua and Caleb might secure passage on one of those ships heading south. There had also been some news that there may be some French warships in the harbor as well. Caleb especially liked the idea. He had always been fascinated by the ships in Boston harbor. The thought of gaining passage on one really intrigued him.

They waited until the end of the week and then went into Boston. John accompanied them; he thought he remembered the best place on the wharf to seek information. As they walked along the half mile long pier, Caleb was again taken by the sight of the ships in the harbor. There were not as

---

1. American Battlefield Trust, Revolutionary War, Charleston the Siege of Charleston

many now since the British warships were gone, but there were still enough to fascinate him. He thought he saw a French warship. It appeared to be flying a French flag. John spotted an older man next to one of the buildings on the pier that he thought he vaguely recognized. They headed toward him. When they got closer, the man called out to them:

"John Reed! Is that you?"

"Yes sir. George," John replied, "it is me."

The man responded, "Why I haven't seen you in forever it seems. How you be?"

"I am fine. This is my son Caleb and his friend Joshua. Caleb, Joshua, I want you to meet an old friend, George Mackle. I used to work with him years ago on the docks."

"Glad to meet you boys." George responded holding out his hand, "John, you still married to that pretty wife of yours; what was her name?"

"Mary. Yes, I am. Got six children now. Caleb is our oldest."

George shaking his head, "Wow! I think your Mary was pregnant with you Caleb the last I time I saw you, John. What brings you here out to the wharf?"

"Caleb and Joshua are seeking passage on a ship heading south."

George looking sternly at the young men, "You boys ain't no Tories, are you? I do not want to help no Tories."

John remembered George as not too fond of the British, so he felt it was safe to reveal that Caleb and Joshua were Continental soldiers.

"No George. My boy and Joshua had been fighting Tories in the Continental army. They came home a while back and now feel they need to get back into the fight."

"Well in that case," George responded in a softer tone, "I will help you all I can. You say you want a ship going south? How far south do you want to go?"

Joshua responded, "We heard that the army was trying to retake Savannah. We thought that may be a good place to see if we can find them."

"Could be difficult down there;" George added with a bit of a scowl, "that is Tory country. I think half the south are our enemies. I used to think we were all Americans. I did not realize so many were traitors."

"I know George," John inserted, "it isn't right that Americans are fighting Americans. I think someday those folks down there will regret siding with the British. If Washington and his army win this war, there may not be any place in the United States where they will be welcome."

"Well, they sure are not going to be welcomed in Boston!" George emphatically emphasized, "You wait here. Let me check around for you on the docks and see what I can find."

"Thank you, George." John responded.

George then headed toward another section of the pier. John and Joshua looked around for a place to sit down. Caleb, still fascinated by the ships, headed toward one that was docked. It was a schooner. He remembered what the sailor told him about the different ships when he first came to the docks. As he approached, one of the sailors stopped him and asked what he wanted. Caleb told him that he was just admiring the ship and that as a younger boy he had always been fascinated by the tall sailing ships. He stuck out his hand and introduced himself to the sailor. The sailor did not respond immediately. It took a bit more talking before Caleb convinced him that he did not have any evil intent.

"Can't be too careful these days. Don't know who you can trust, although it is a little better since most of the loyalists have left. My name is John Fargo. Glad to meet you, Caleb."

He stuck out his hand and Caleb shook it. Caleb asked several questions about a schooner ship and how it differed from a frigate warship. The sailor soon realized he was dealing with a novice about sailing, but he always liked to show off his knowledge of the sea, so he answered every question and even explained some of the basics of sailing. Caleb listened intently, hanging on to every word.

At one point, Caleb asked John, the sailor, about the knot used to secure the ship.

"That big iron thing the rope is around is a cleat. The rope is wrapped that way so that it will not come loose if the wind picks up and the ships pulls on it. When pulled, the knot gets tighter, but if you ease up on it, you can untie it quickly when the ship is ready to leave."

John then picked up a smaller diameter rope.

"Ropes are very important to seamen." Sailor John told him. "They hold things in place, allow you to control the sails, and a host of other things. They can even save your life. Being at sea is not like being on dry land. The deck is always moving. You must learn how to walk on it and sometimes it isn't easy. If the wind is up or in storm conditions, it is even harder. A rope secured to something may be the only way you can move around. Every sailor knows when the sea is up, he must hang on to something all the time."

Caleb eyes wide, "Wow! I had not thought about that."

John asked, "Do you know how to tie a bowline knot?"

"No." Caleb responded.

"Let me show you." Picking up a piece of rope. "That knot is one of the first knots a sailor learns to tie because it could save his life. Let's suppose you are hanging on to something on the ship and another person throws you a lifeline. You must keep hanging on, but somehow you need to work the lifeline around you and tie a knot in it so you can be pulled to safety. You only have one hand free, and you do not want to tie a knot that will slip on you. If it does, your insides could be crushed as others try to pull you to safety. You understand the situation?"

Joshua nodded with fascination. John then threw the end of the rope to him. He told him to grab the rope up a ways, and he would show him how to tie a bowline knot to secure the end of the rope around him.

John emphasized, "Now do not let go of the rope in your left hand. Use your other hand to bring the rope around you and then grab the very end of it. With the rope in your right hand, place your hand over the rope between your body and your left hand. Now work your right hand around the left rope so that a loop forms around your right hand. Now take the end of the rope and push it around the part of the rope above your right hand, catch it on the other side and pull it down through the loop around your wrist. Now pull the end of the rope down so the loop falls off your right hand and then pull the end as tight as you can. The knot should tighten but not slip."

Caleb did well the first time. He tried it again to make sure. Afterwards, he untied the rope and gave it back to John. He thanked him for the lesson, the information and headed back to his father and Joshua. When he got to them, he beamed.

Caleb with a proud smile, "I just learned to tie a bowline knot!"

It was the better part of an hour before George returned. He had found a schooner called "The Rachel" owned by the Adams family, well known Patriots. That ship would take them aboard and help them get to their destination, but they would not be sailing until about noon the next day when the tide was right. George wrote down the information. They all thanked George for his help. He wished them Godspeed, and they headed back home to prepare for the journey.

When they got back, they all decided to share supper together so everyone could say their goodbyes. They all knew they needed to go, but no one was happy about it. After supper, Sarah took Joshua by the hand and led him outside to the other side of the barn next to the house. There was a spot there where she knew they could be alone. She then put her hand on his arm as she often did and said with tears in her eyes that she would miss him terribly. Her hand felt warm, but he did not want her to cry. She then hugged him, hard. He put his hands around her and returned the hug. This felt different to him. She was trying to tell him something, but he did not know what it was. She then pulled away and looked into his eyes. Realizing he still did not get it; she grabbed his face and kissed him long on the lips. Afterwards she pulled away and saw the shocked look on his face.

Sarah expressing her thoughts, "Why are men so dumb when it comes to relationships? Joshua Rutledge, I love you! Is that plain enough for you."

Joshua was stunned but also felt terrible. Her kiss was a shock but also pleasant. Did he love her too? He thought of his feeling for Jessica. Sarah could see his confusion; she could read him well. She knew what he was thinking. She also knew about Jessica. Caleb had told her about the girl in Boston. She could see he was wrestling with his emotions and did not know where she stood within them. She had to let him know how she felt. She had been pushing clues his way for a while, but men do not seem to pick up on things that women think ought to be obvious. She knew he was leaving, and this would be her last chance but now she had to let him go, hope he would be alright, and return safe. Only time would tell whether he would return to her or Jessica. She turned and walked away. He had the urge to follow her, but something told him that was not what she wanted, at least not now.

Unbeknownst to Sarah, Hannah took Caleb aside and did almost the same thing to him. The girls had talked to each other about how they felt. Sarah had even encouraged Hannah to let Caleb know how she felt. She had watched Sarah approach Joshua and had learned. The two young women, for that is what they were now, would console each other and grieve together as the loves of their life left for war. They would pray for them for safety and a safe return, each hoping for something else.

Joshua and Caleb said their goodbyes the night before so they could be up before sunrise. They wanted to make sure they allowed enough time to make it to the ship. Thomas and John were up early as was their custom, so they each bid farewell to their sons and follow part of the way with them. Then they watched for a while. Each man prayed for his son and his son's friend. Then each man turned to go back home saddened to have to send them off to war again.

Chapter 13

Voyage

Joshua and Caleb reached the ship well before noon. A sailor named Jack came off the Rachel and greeted them.

"My name is Jack."

Joshua and Caleb introduced themselves.

Jack asked, "Ever been aboard a sailing ship before?"

Both young men answered, "no!"

Jack motioned toward the gangplank, "Let me take you to your bunks and then I will give you a quick tour of the Rachel."

He led them aboard and guided them down below to a small area with two bunks where they could stow their things.

"Space is precious aboard a sailing ship," Jack advised, "so we use every available space as best we can. You will just have to get use to the cramped quarters."

He then led them up a ladder to the main deck.

Jack led them up the ladder, "When aboard a ship, always hang onto something like this rail along the ladder. We are docked now, and everything is stable like on land. At sea the ship is constantly moving. If you do not hang on, you could get hurt."

Joshua and Caleb shook their heads so that he knew they understood.

Jack pointing to the mast, "When the sails are up, there will be a lot of things happening on the main deck, raising and lowering the sails, trimming them for the wind conditions, and so forth. Please stay back aft when all that is happening."

Caleb was puzzled, "Aft?"

"Oh, you boys are new to sailing, aren't you." Jack responded. "Ok, let me give some quick sailing terms. The front of the boat is the bow. The back is the stern. Going aft means going toward the stern, going forward toward the bow. We also have terms for right and left. Facing the bow, the right side of the boat is referred to as starboard and the left side as port. There are also all kinds of terms for the kind of sails and parts of the sails, but you do not need to know that. We sailors will take care of sailing her. Do you understand?"

Both shook their heads, "Yes"

Jack added, "We will likely leave in about a half an hour, so you boys get settled. If you would like to know a bit more about how we sail her, at least the basics, I will be happy to teach you later after we are out to sea. Til then, you can go below and explore a bit. I will catch up with you later."

Joshua and Caleb thanked him. He seemed to like sharing his knowledge of the sea with them. They went below and explored for a bit. Then they felt the ship beginning to move and went back up on deck to watch. The lines to the dock had been removed and "stowed", another term they would learn later meant put away. There were other lines attached to the ship, and then out to a couple of rowboats. Caleb had seen this before. The rowboats were pulling the ship away from the dock into deeper water. He surmised they needed deeper water and more room before they could put up the sails. They both watched, fascinated.

After about an hour or so of maneuvering out of the harbor and around some obstacles, they were under way under full sail. It was Caleb that noticed, however, that they appeared to be heading north not south as they expected. They saw Jack and asked him about it.

"Yeah, we are heading north or more specifically a little northeast." Jack explained, "We are going to go up to Halifax first before we head south for several reasons. Out here in the ocean we are in a kind of current that runs northward. We will make better time using that current. There are also British warships aplenty immediately to the south and we want to avoid them if possible. We have some supplies that we will unload at Halifax and take on some more at that port. Then we will head south but further offshore beyond the north ward current, so we do not have to fight it going south. It is likely that there will be fewer warships out there as well."

It all made sense to Joshua and Caleb. They now had another problem they had not anticipated. Their stomachs were acting up. Jack saw that they were looking a "little green" as sailors described it. He had anticipated it. He told them they were seasick. He told them to concentrate on the horizon, and he gave them a little bread for their stomachs. He told them that after a time, they would get their "sea legs" and things would be better. Joshua and Caleb were not so sure about that. They rushed to the railing on the side of the ship and emptied their stomachs over the side. Jack gave them more bread and told them to fight it.

They were sick most of the afternoon and finally began to feel better. They were getting their "sea legs". They got some more bread in them, which is all they wanted for supper. They finally retired to their assigned bunk later and slept through the night. The next morning, they felt much better. They moved around and talked with some of the others in the crew. They learned a little more about the schooner. It was about seventy-five feet long and about twenty-two feet wide. Her draft was about nine feet. Her crew was about forty men.

It took about three days or so to reach Halifax and dock. Joshua and Caleb deboarded the schooner to look around. When they did, they found that the dock felt like it was moving. Jack laughed as they he saw them.

"Don't worry boys," Jack said to take off the edge, "the ground will stop moving in a bit. Just like your body will get used to being on a ship, it also must get used to being back on land again."

Jack told them that they would likely leave in two days. It would take a little time to unload the ship and reload with new supplies. They decided to explore the port.

"Be careful boys," Jack cautioned, "do not let it be known that you are a Patriot and were soldiers in the Continental army. A lot of the loyalists moved here after the war started. It was also rebels that raided this port for the Patriot cause. You will not be well received. They may even try to hang you if they find out, so be careful. You need to look like you are loyal to England and just trying to get away from the war. Got it?"

Joshua and Caleb responded, "Got it."

They moved down the dock and walked around a bit. The port was large. Joshua and Caleb would not be able to see it all. There were taverns like in Boston and some shops. Time passed, they became hungry and decided to stop at a tavern for some food. They were glad they still had the English pounds their parents had given them. They did not want to show any rebel currency. They could break one of the pound notes and buy enough food for them both.

After eating they came upon a dry goods store that looked vaguely familiar. They stepped onto the porch and then discovered why. Inside Joshua saw a very familiar figure. It was Jessica. She saw him at the same moment and almost dropped what she was holding. She quickly finished with an apparent customer and then came out to him and saw Caleb as well.

Jessica in a whisper, "Joshua, what on earth are you doing here?" It isn't safe for you here, either of you."

Joshua also lowering his voice, "We are just passing through. We just arrived on a schooner this morning and we are going to leave in two days. We did not even know you were here."

Jessica was glad to see him and glad he was alright, but she was also fearful that others around might find out who they were. Another young man who seemed to be a little protective of her came out to see what these two young men wanted with her and how she knew them. Jessica quickly said that she knew them back in Boston and that they, like she and her father, had finally escaped from there when the rebels took over. She told him that their families had been regular customers at her father's store and that is how she knew them. It was not totally true but that was all that she could think of at that moment. She wanted to just grab Joshua and hug him and then maybe slap him for making her worry so much. She refrained, she must give the impression that they were just acquaintances and that was all.

Jessica greeted them, "Well, Mr. Rutledge, I believe that is your name, isn't it?"

Joshua nodded.

Jessica turning her attention to Caleb, "I think I remember your family name was Steed. Wasn't it?"

Caleb began to catch on to what she was doing, "No, it is Reed."

"Oh yes, now I remember."

She then asked a series of questions designed to convince, what appeared to be a young suitor, that these men were just former acquaintances of her father and her from Boston.

Jessica in a polite voice designed to convince listeners she was speaking to old but not close acquaintances, "How are you both?"

Both responded in unison: "Fine"

Jessica continued, "And how are your families?"

They added, "They are well."

"Will you be with us long?" Jessica asked.

Caleb interjected, "Just a day or so; we will be sailing I believe the day after tomorrow."

Jessica wanted to know the ship that had brought them to Halifax so she could meet Joshua later but did not want to make that fact obvious.

"Well, I hope the ship is a good ship and that brought you to us."

Caleb caught on to what she wanted to know; Joshua was still too shocked.

Caleb responded, "Yes, it was a schooner called the Rachel. I had not been aboard a ship before, but I have always been fascinated with the sea. This trip has been a treat for me."

Jessica added, "Well I hope you did not get seasick like I did when we came up."

"Oh no;" Caleb lied, "I got my sea legs right away."

Joshua was about to say something, but Jessica cut him off.

Jessica ended the conversation, "Well, I must go back inside; there are more customers you know. I am glad to see you again."

She then quickly shook both of their hands and turned around and went back in the store, she would find the ship later. Her protector was apparently satisfied that these were just old customers nothing more and followed her back inside.

Joshua and Caleb walked away. Joshua was stunned to have found her. Was this a sign from God. She was just as beautiful as he remembered. He remembered the times they spent together, her mannerisms, her cute expressions. Then Sarah came to his mind.

"She will find us. Are you going to tell her about my sister?" Caleb asked.

Joshua hung his head, "I think I must. It would not be right to keep that from her."

Caleb: added, "You know that Sarah already knows about Jessica."

Joshua surprised and puzzled, "How does she know?"

"Come on Josh," Caleb frowning a bit, "I spilled the beans when you first met Jessica. Sarah has asked about her ever since."

It finally dawned on Joshua why Sarah had acted the way she did the night before he left. She was putting in her bid for his affection knowing that there was another girl in the picture. Joshua knew that at some point; he would have to make a choice. He knew that he loved Jessica but that kiss from Sarah was ... well, something too. He would never want to hurt either of them.

They found their way back to the ship. Joshua pondered his dilemma for a while. He waited but Jessica did not come that evening. They both finally went down to their bunks to sleep.

The next morning, they helped the sailors unload and load supplies. About noon Jessica came walking toward the ship. Jack first spotted her.

Jack noticing Jessica, "Whoa, where did this pretty lady come from and who for?"

Jessica heard him and smiled slightly; she liked the attention. She came straight up to Joshua and kissed him like she wanted to the day before. Then she stepped back and slapped like she wanted to the day before. Joshua was stunned. He never quite knew what to expect from her.

Jack exclaimed, "Wow, Joshua, you haven't been one day in port, and you already have a girlfriend, and she is already mad at you. You move fast, maybe too fast."

Jessica then turned toward Jack and held out her hand, "I am Jessica, and no Joshua did not get himself a girlfriend overnight. We have known each other for several years and we met in Boston. The kiss was to show I care about him, the slap was to show how much I am angry with him for making me worry so much."

Jack took her hand a little startled and replied, "I am pleased to meet you, Jessica. I am Jack, one of the crew on the Rachel."

Jack eyes wide, "Wow, Josh, you have a real firebrand there, a real pretty one at that."

Jessica smiled slightly, "Is there somewhere where Joshua and I can talk privately."

Jack accommodated her request, "Josh, take her down to the rear cabin on the ship. Most of the crew have gone into town now and won't be back 'til supper. That should be private."

She thanked him. And Joshua led her onto the ship and down an aft ladder to the cabin. There was a table there and some chairs. She did not sit down right away. She came over to Joshua and hugged him, hard. She then kissed him, a long kiss like the one that Sarah had given him. When she pulled away, there were tears in her eyes. That broke Joshua's heart. They both tried to speak at the same time at that point.

Joshua insisted, "You first."

Jessica then told him all that had happened since leaving Boston. She told him she was sorry for deceiving him before she left but she had to leave with her father. She just couldn't bring herself to tell him face to face that she had to leave. She told him she had been thinking about him all the time.

Jessica touched his face, "I love you, Joshua. I was worried about you. Were you Ok? Were you hurt? I do not think I would have been able to take it if you had been killed. I did try to write you."

Joshua responded, "I know, I got the letter. I still have it."

"Did you write back?" The she remembered, "Wait, of course you did, I got one from you. I think that was the only one though."

"I know, I am sorry." Joshua apologized, "I am just not that good at writing. Those last two winters, Valley Forge and Morristown were horrible. I have never been so cold. Men were dying in camp. There wasn't enough food, shoes, blankets, and other supplies. I guess I did not want you to hear about all that."

"I just wanted to hear from you, Joshua." she answered emphatically, "Something, anything."

Joshua hung his head, "I am sorry."

Jessica knew he meant it. She forgave him and then came over and hugged him again. They talked for a while longer, but she knew something was different. She could not determine exactly what, but something was different.

"Joshua, I know you want to tell me something." Jessica insisted, "What is it?"

Joshua did not know how to begin, so he told her about being very sick this winter in camp, Caleb too. When they finally felt better, they both asked if they could take leave and go back home. They were told it would be ok. He told her about the trip back, how they made it across the Hudson River undetected. He told her about the two farmers that took them part way and then gave them two horses to carry them the rest of the way. That had been a real blessing. He told her how happy everyone was to see them. There were a lot of hugs....and kisses. When he said that and how he said it Jessica's antenna perked up. She knew he was very close to telling her something.

Joshua continued, "You know that Caleb and I have been friends all our lives."

"Yes."

Joshua added, "Our families have been close. We all grew up together. Things changed too as we got older. My sister Hannah really likes Caleb. I think she is in love with him."

Jessicas senses were on high alert, "Does Caleb have a sister too?"

Joshua hung his head, "Yes."

"Is she in love with you, Josh?" Jessica asked.

Joshua responded, "Yes."

Jessica put her hands on his face, lifted his head, and looked him straight in his eyes, "Do you love her?"

Tears started down Joshuas face; he could not hold them back.

"I think so, but I love you too."

He looked at her with a forlorn "what do I do?" expression.

Jessica in an angry voice, "Did you seduce her Joshua, like Jack indicated, a girl in every port?"

"No, no, it was never like that." Joshua insisted, "She is part of my family. I would never do that to a woman. Jessica, you know me."

She knew he was telling the truth; she could see it in his face. He was being pulled apart.

Jessica said sternly, "I think I have the right to know her name, Joshua."

Joshua responded, "Sarah, she is a couple of years younger than Caleb and I."

Jessica looked him square in his eyes again.

"You know you will have to make a choice."

"I know but how do I choose," Joshua insisted, "I think I am in love with you both and it is tearing me apart. You know me Jessica and that I am telling you the truth."

She did; he could never really hide anything from her. It was one of the things she loved about him. She would have to meet this, Sarah.

Joshua in a lower forlorn voice, "We are going back to the fight tomorrow. Maybe that will solve everything."

A shocked Jessica scolded, "Joshua Rutledge, do not say such things! Do you think getting yourself killed will solve the problem? Do you want both our hearts broken?"

"No, no, I am sorry. That was stupid." Joshua hung his head gain.

Jessica agreed, "Yes."

She knew Joshua. She could always read him well. She could see he was agonizing over the dilemma. She was angry and at the same time felt a little sorry for him. His pain confirmed to her that he did in fact still love her. If he did not it would still have been an awkward moment but not a difficult choice. She decided to leave him with one last bid for his affection. After some reflection, she stood up, came over, hugged him, and kissed him. She then told him that she loved him. It was a scene reminiscent of the one he had with Sarah. Without saying anything more, she climbed up to the deck, left the ship, and headed back. Joshua followed her up but did not leave the ship. He just watched deep in thought as she walked away.

The schooner sailed the next day. Joshua was quiet. Caleb, on the other hand, was anxious to learn more about sailing. Jack was happy to oblige. He liked showing his knowledge of the sea. Jack quickly determined that Caleb knew very little about how a sailing vessel operates, so he made a small model of a simple sailing vessel. He took a piece of wood to represent the hull, dug a hole in its center and put a stick in it to represent a mast, and tied a piece of cloth onto the stick to represent a sail. He then added a thin piece of wood lengthwise on the bottom of the "hull" to represent a keel. He explained each part as he was assembling it. He then added a piece of string to the top of the mast.

Jack asked, "Do you know what that is for?"

Caleb answered, "No."

"The driving force on a sailing ship is the wind." Jack continued switching to his teaching voice, "A sailor must always be aware of the wind direction to effectively sail the ship. At top of the main mast on this ship (he pointed up to it) you will find a piece of cloth or streamer, clearly visible from the deck. The wind will blow that cloth out from the mast in the direction that the wind is heading. That is how we determine the wind direction. We must always be aware of that. How we set the sails to take advantage of the wind depends on the wind direction and what direction we want the ship to go." Caleb nodded that he understood.

Jack added, "Right here on the deck is a compass. The needle on it always points north. Knowing that, can you figure out which direction the wind is blowing right now?"

Caleb pointed toward the stern, "Let's see, the compass indicates north is behind us, therefore we are heading south. The streamer points off the starboard side, so that would be southwest."

Jack praised him, "Very good Caleb." We will make a sailor out of you yet! When the wind flows over the sails, there are two forces on the ship. One tries to move the ship in the direction of the wind, in this case southwest. There is also a forward force to move the ship in the direction the bow is headed. Which brings me to the bottom part of this model, the keel. Without the keel, the ship would mostly move with the wind, sideways. Notice the keel is thin along one axis, the ship axis, but thick when viewed from the side. The keel provides heavy resistance to the sideways motion but minimal resistance to the forward motion. The sail and the keel together allow us to move the ship in the direction we wish. Does all this make sense, Caleb?"

Caleb pondered the lesson for a moment,

"Yes."

"We also need to 'trim' the sails." Jack continued, "That means to adjust the angle of the sails with respect to the wind. Each angle produces a corresponding sideways force and a forward force. The idea is to adjust the angle so that the forward force is maximized, and the sideways force is minimized. If the wind changes, the sails will need to be readjusted or trimmed. If we wish to travel in a different direction, the sails will need to be readjusted. In fact, the sails will need to be continually adjusted during a turn to maintain a smooth turn and continuous control. There is always a part of the crew on deck working together to make sure everything happens correctly."

Caleb a bit surprised, "Wow, there is more to this sailing then I thought."

Jack added, "I am going to draw you a little sketch based on our little model and wind direction to illustrate how the sails would be set when traveling at different angles with respect to the wind."

Caleb: "Thanks."

Jack: "Oh, one more thing, we cannot sail directly into the wind. That would stop the ship's forward motion and push it backwards. What we must do to move the ship into the wind is travel at an angle into the wind for a while and then shift to the opposite side for a while. It is done repeatedly into the wind and is known as tacking."

Jack used the model to illustrate what he was saying. When he saw that Caleb was getting the idea, he left to complete his drawing. He came back later and gave the drawing to him and told him to study it and watch as the crew sailed the ship.

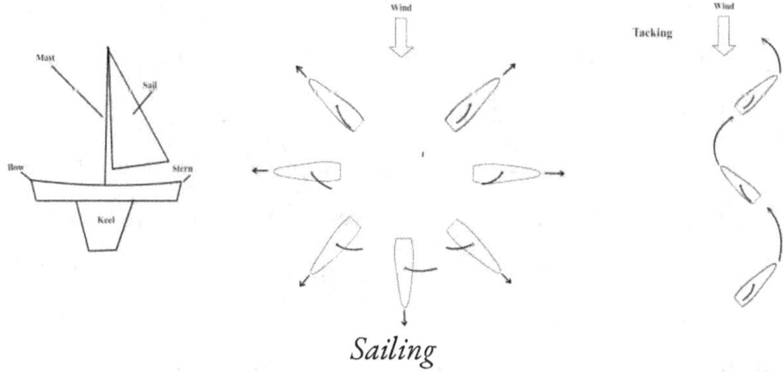

Sailing

They were at sea ten days by the time they were off the southern coast of South Carolina. The winds had been favorable, and they did not run into any British warships. Now, however, they need to be more cautious. The closer they came to Charleston, now under British control, the more likely they would run into trouble. Jack told them that they might land them at a beach north of Charleston called Myrtle Beach. They chose Myrtle Beach because the land there was higher going inland. Around Charleston and further south there were a lot of lowland swamps and at this time of the year, a whole lot of bugs. From there they would have to move carefully inland to seek the Patriot forces. It would be hard. There were a lot of loyalists in the south, and it might be difficult to tell friend from foe. Jack added they were welcome to any supplies, food, and ammunition that they thought they could carry. Joshua and Caleb thought it was a good plan.

When they came closer to land, they spotted a tall mast on the horizon. They could not see the ship yet or the colors she was flying. They decided to watch a bit to see which way she was heading. If it was a warship, it was likely they had not seen them yet. Their mast was taller than the Rachel's and would show above the curvature of the earth first. If it was a smaller ship, it would likely be a merchant ship and not a danger.

They watched for about an hour and decided the ship was coming towards them; the mast was growing taller. They hoped they still had not yet been seen but to be a little safer, the captain decided to move in closer to shore. They would be no match for a British warship; they only had two small cannons on board. The captain knew the area well. There were a couple of shallower areas that would be a problem for a warship with a deeper draft. If they were closer in and were spotted, they might be able to make a run for the shallows. If the warship followed, she might well run aground. In the open ocean, the warship might be able to overtake them, especially since the wind had shifted to a more southerly breeze. A warship carries a lot more sail than the Rachel and that could mean greater speed. The captain ordered a change of course. They watched the mast grow as the ship came closer and closer. The tension mounted over the next hour and after that they still had not yet seen any signs of the shoreline.

After another hour, a lookout called out that he had spotted land. The other ship was now close enough for the captain to make out the ship's colors with a spyglass. She was a warship; the tension mounted. Joshua and Caleb grew a little nervous. Caleb especially had seen a warship up close. They looked formidable with forty cannons on each side on a lower deck and more placed elsewhere. She could blow them out of the water if she was a mind to. Minute by minute the warship came closer and closer but so did the land. It was a race. The men were silent. The tension mounted. Joshua and Caleb gripped the railing on the ship tighter and tighter. When they were about three miles off the beach, the captain saw a change in the warship; she seemed to be turning. At first, he did not know whether they had spotted them and were now turning toward them or something else. The next half hour would make it clear. The minutes ticked on. Five minutes, then ten, then fifteen; at twenty minutes a crew member called out.

Sailor responded excitedly, "She's turning away, captain, she's turning away."

The captain watched with his spyglass for confirmation.

Captain agreed, "Yep, she's turning away"

They would never know whether the warship had spotted them and decided that they were of no interest or had not seen them and merely changed course for a totally different reason. In any case everyone breathed a sigh of relief.

Captain added, "God must be with you boys."

The Rachel was anchored off the coast and Joshua and Caleb were taken to the beach on a rowboat. They thanked everyone, especially Jack and the captain. They waved goodbye and headed inland. They needed to be especially watchful. There were no badges on people identifying those that would be friendly to them. They could not even trust the women and children. Some may be loyalists, and they would not take kindly to Patriots.

They moved inland as quietly as they could while keeping a sharp lookout for the telltale red uniforms of the British soldiers and officers. They thought that would be a sure sign they were approaching the enemy. It would be a little harder to determine a Patriot militia, although, they felt that any leaders would probably not be wearing red uniforms. They also prayed that they would find the militia God wanted them to join.

They dodged a couple of patrols that looked like they might be loyalists as they moved inland. Fortunately, there was no lack of water. It was July so there were some berries and some fruit to be had if they were careful not to be seen. Midday, temperatures seemed hotter than what they were used to in Boston. They found a place to hide and dozed off. When the sun was no longer directly overhead, they would venture on.

About ten days inland, they came upon a promising group of soldiers. There were no redcoats and many of them looked like mountain men, full beards, and clothes appeared to be made from animal skins. Quite a few of them had longer rifles, different than the muskets they were used to. They decided to carefully move in close enough to hear their conversations. It was evening. They overheard them talking about the blue ridge mountains, Tennessee, and Kentucky, confirming that these were indeed mountain men.

They decided to wait until the next day to make contact; they did not want to be mistaken for a loyalist and shot. The next morning, they came out of hiding with their muskets on their backs in an unthreatening manner and they were able to make contact. The militia was indeed a Patriot force under the command of General Sumter. Joshua and Caleb identified themselves and told their story. The men could tell that they were not from the south. An officer that had been in the Morristown camp where Washington wintered with his men, was with them. A few questions to Joshua and Caleb convinced him that they were telling the truth, and they had been at Morristown. After that they were welcomed.

Joshua asked, "Where exactly are we? We have been walking for days from the coast, but we are not sure how far we have come."

Mountain Man answered, "We are near the town of Kershaw, South Carolina. My name is Benjamin, and I am from Tennessee."

Joshua held out his hand, "Glad to meet you, Benjamin."

Caleb did the same, "Me too Benjamin."

Joshua noticing his rifle, "That is a mighty fine rifle you have. I don't think I have seen one like that.

We were only given these muskets."

Benjamin explained, "There are a lot of these where we come from; most mountain men want to have one.

"What makes it so special?" Joshua inquired,

"See the long barrel." Benjamin pointed, "The inside is bored out making the lead ball spin as it exits. The rifle also uses more powder and the way we put the ball in there is less blast leakage around the ball."

Joshua looked a little confused.

Benjamin explained, "All of that makes the ball come out faster and travel further."

"How far?" Joshua asked.

Benjamin answered, "Well, I have killed game with it at up to three hundred yards."

Joshua and Caleb's eye got wide at that.

Both exclaimed, "Wow!"

Caleb added, "Come to think of it, I think I heard about a gun like that.

Now I get to see one!"

"There are a few up north too," Benjamin continued, "mostly again owned by mountain men. Many of us make a living by trapping and killing game for their hides. Some of the furs bring good money. We need to shoot accurate sometimes at a good distance. If we get too close, the game detects us and runs away. If we are not accurate, we may just wound the animal. A wounded animal can sometime cover a great distance before it goes down. If that happens, we will likely never find it. We mountain men get pretty good at shooting. If we didn't, we would starve."

The men made Joshua and Caleb feel at home and they officially became part of their Mountain men militia.

Chapter 14
Strategies

Henry Clinton, the British General, decided that the weakest part of the American defenses was in the south. It was in the south where the loyalist support was the strongest. The British had decided that the best way to fight Americans is with other Americans. He felt they did not need to bring more troops from England, just get the gullible Americans to fight for them. He appointed Charles Lord Cornwallis to head up the southern campaign. The plan was to capture the main ports. They had already captured Savannah, they now set their sights on Charleston, South Carolina. With these two ports added to the port in New York City, they felt they could control much of the eastern seaboard. They would have to bring in supplies for their troops and at the same time cut off supplies to the rebels. Then they would march the army up from Georgia, through the Carolinas to Virginia.

They felt at that point; they would have Washington at their mercy and force this upstart general and his ragtag backwoods army to capitulate.

They had not counted on the determination of Washington's army, nor the fact that they were now hardened into a significant fighting force. Washington had put Nathanael Greene in charge of the southern forces. There were also those mountain men from the western areas.

At first, things seemed to be going their way. They already occupied

Savannah, and the American forces were unable to recapture that port in the fall of 1779. Those forces had retreated to Charleston, only to later surrender. The British now controlled three critical ports, New York City, Charleston, and Savannah. With those ports and the substantial fleet of warships and supply ships, Cornwallis was confident he could control the eastern seacoast and supply the needs of his army as they prepared to conquer Georgia and the Carolinas.

With the first phase now accomplished, Cornwallis is now set upon executing the second phase, recruiting loyalists to fight against the rebels.

At the end of May, the British overwhelmed a small Patriot force at the Battle of Waxhaws, South Carolina. Survivors reported that the British massacred many men who tried to surrender. The Patriots used the event as a propaganda victory to stir up anti-British sentiment with the slogan "Remember Waxhaws". [1]

In June, there was fierce fighting between recruited loyalists and Patriots at Ramseur's Mill, North Carolina. It did not go as Cornwallis hoped. The loyalists were overwhelmed, and loyalist morale plummeted. [2]

It was also in June that Washington's army left Morristown, New Jersey. Some weeks later, French troops arrived at Newport, Rhode Island, but were not really used until almost a year later. Washington leaves the hands-on leadership of the army to his generals, particularly Nathanael Greene, to deal with Cornwallis in the south. He may have felt he needed to shore up better support for the army and better treatment for civilians,

---

1. American Battlefield Trust, Revolutionary War, Waxhaws Buford's Massacre

2. American History Central, Battle of Ramsour's Mill – A critical American Victory in North Carolina.

some of which had been ravaged for supplies.

Greene's army of Patriots had been through tough times and had learned a few things along the way. They learned, for example, you did not have to win every battle to further the cause. They just needed to wear down the enemy. They were largely fighting other Americans, loyalists. If Greene's army could inflict enough casualties and destroy the morale of these loyalists, they may well give up the fight. The British soldiers would not be able to maintain the war with just the British troops. It had already cost the crown too much. Great Britain also now had two new old foes joining in the conflict, France and Spain. Spain was attacking southern ports gaining an increased foothold in the south.

The French had sent two fleets of warships, one of which the British had yet to engage. They knew the French were quite capable at sea with battle prowess comparable to their own. If they did not decisively win the war soon, they may never win it. If the American Patriots could just hold out. They had fought for years now. There was battle fatigue but there also was a great deal of determination. Freedom was at stake, and they did not want to again be under the British tyranny.

To accomplish the goal, Greene incorporated two tactics. One was a hit and run tactic. They would strike at the enemy and then scatter in the surrounding woods. It annoyed the British and exasperated the loyalists but each time more loyalists and some British troops were added to the casualty list. They would also attack small outposts. The idea was to harass the enemy enough and deplete their supplies to make them think maintaining the outpost was unsustainable. The Battle of Hanging Rock, South Carolina was one of those outposts. In August 1780, Patriot forces under General Thomas Sumter fought and then withdrew but were able to achieve their purpose. Many loyalists fled and Sumter was able to capture 100 horses, 250 muskets, some supplies, and seventy-three prisoners.

It was considered an American victory. It would have been one of the better-known victories had Sumter chased them out of Hanging Rock. [3] Joshua and Caleb participated in this battle after joining up with Sumter's Mountain men.

There was another such battle about ten days later at Musgrove Mill, South Carolina. It was a local grain supply and the site of a Tory (loyalist) outpost. A Patriot force got word from a friendly farmer that the post had been reinforced. Rather than attack, they quietly set up battle positions on a ridge overlooking the mill. A small detachment was then sent out to lure the loyalists out into a trap. The Tories fought with fixed bayonets and at first the patriot militia was forced back. Another Patriot militia came and engaged in the fight and wounded the Tory leader. The Tories retreated after suffering heavy casualties. The Patriot losses were light. [4]

Not all battles went to the Patriots. On the same day as the Musgrove Mill battle, The Patriots general, Gates, leading the Patriots made a critical error against the British troops under Cornwallis at Camden, South Carolina. It was tradition that when lining up troops to face the enemy, the more experienced troops would be placed on the right. Gates should have lined up his most experienced men on his left to face the experienced troops of Cornwallis. He did the opposite so that Cornwallis's experienced troops were able to overrun the lesser experienced troops of Gates. Gates had to retreat. That defeat reassured Cornwallis that the weak part of the Patriot forces was indeed in the south, and he could continue to attack up through the Carolinas.

Cornwallis had not yet met the mountain boys of Kentucky and Ten-

---

3. American Battlefield Trust, Revolutionary War, Hanging Rock

4. American Battlefield Trust, Revolutionary War, Musgrove Mill.

nessee. Many of them were fur traders and made their living from hunting and trapping among other things. Besides being just plain tough, they also had a kind of secret weapon that was not as well known in the north or by the British. It was the Kentucky Long Rifle, the same one that Benjamin had shown Joshua and Caleb.

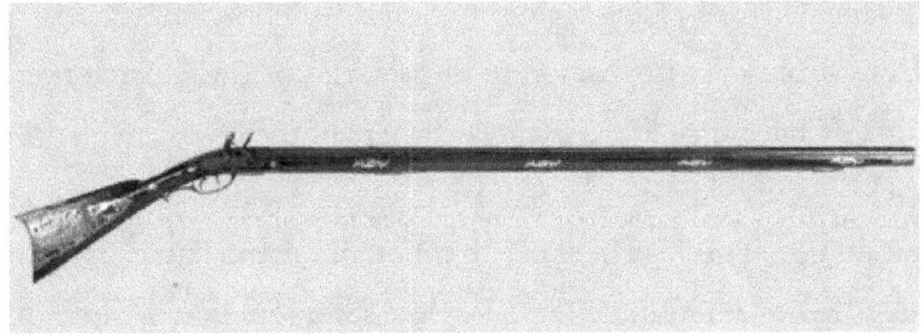

Kentucky Long Rifle

Muskets were accurate to about one hundred yards, although some felt not even that far. The Kentucky rifle was considered accurate to an incredible two-hundred-fifty yards. There were some stories of targets being hit at even three hundred yards. Snipers using the rifle were employed to pick off special targets, usually officers often on horseback. It was a formidable weapon. It had a downside; however, it took a long time to reload compared to the standard musket. It also could not take a bayonet. An enemy charge would likely overrun the shooter. If they did, the rifle was nothing more than a club against a musket with a bayonet which could be wielded like a spear or a sword. To protect the Revolutionary war sniper, he would be surrounded by soldiers with muskets. The rifle struck fear in the hearts of soldiers who had witnessed the lethal angry wasp-like sound the lead ball made traveling through the air. [5]

---

5. Revolutionary War Journal, Muskets & Rifles of the American Revolution: Difference and Tactics.

The mountain men made their living with their rifles. They had to be able to take down the game with a single shot. They had to become expert marksmen. Those were the kind of men the British led loyalist forces were about to face at Kings Mountain, South Carolina.

They were led by Major Patrick Ferguson. He underestimated the mountain men even telling them in typical British bravado:

"Desist from their opposition to British arms or I will march over the mountains, hang their leaders, and lay their country to waste with fire and sword."

You do not say things like that to mountain men. Those are fighting words as Major Ferguson and the loyalists soon found out. The Patriots attacked Ferguson's position from all sides. He, himself was shot off his horse and killed. The loyalists were soundly routed. It also proved that the American riflemen could fire, retreat and reload quick enough to foil an enemy charge. The Battle of Kings Mountain changed things. Cornwallis was no longer as confident in his assessment that the key to defeating Washington was up through the south. In fact, he may well have realized he was now facing Washington's greatest strength rather than his greatest weakness.[6]

A second method incorporated by the Patriots was more elaborate. They would place a line of men facing the enemy to repulse an enemy attack. Hidden about four hundred yards behind them would be a second line. A third line may also be used perhaps another four hundred yards or so behind them. The second and third lines would be kept hidden. When the loyalist attacked the first line, the men on the first line were to fire a couple of times at the loyalists and then turn and run toward the second line. They

---

6. American Battlefield Trust, Revolutionary War, Kings Mountain

were trying to create the illusion that the Patriots were panicking, which had happened in the past, and lure the loyalists into charging them. When the loyalists had now run across four hundred yards, they would suddenly find themselves facing brutal fire from the second line. Meanwhile, the first line could attempt to reload and join in the fire. If they then managed to charge through the second line, then they would face even more accurate fire from the most seasoned troops in the third line.

In January 1781, Nathanael Greene who, in the fall had been made commander of the southern Continental army, was sent to thwart Cornwallis. Greene dispatched over a one thousand Patriots under Brigadier General Daniel Morgan to the Catawba River to cut British supply lines. Cornwallis sent an equal number of troops under Lieutenant Colonel Banastre Tarleton to counter Morgan.

Tarleton had a brutal reputation for allowing his forces to massacre Americans who tried to surrender. Tarleton chased Morgan and they finally confronted each other at Cowpens, South Carolina. Tarleton did not have good intelligence on the American forces. Morgan used the technique of putting a line of men out front and then a second line hidden behind. The front line was to fire a couple of volleys and then retreat.

Tarleton was fooled into thinking the Americans had panicked and he ordered his men to chase them. They ran into a brutal line of fire from the mountain rifle men. Then they were attacked by a calvary unit led by William Washington, a distant cousin of George Washington. The British were soundly routed. That defeat forced Cornwallis to give up his effort to take South Carolina. [7]

Instead, he moved to North Carolina. On February 1, at Cowan's Ford

---

7. American Battlefield Trust, Revolutionary War, Cowpens

on the Catawba River in Northwestern North Carolina, British forces of about five thousand were pitted against a thousand Americans. Cornwallis planned a three-pronged attack to overpower the Americans. He ordered the capture of Wilmington as a port for supplies. He sent troops to Charlotte as his main body and sent Partick Ferguson west to enlist Tory support. Five weeks later everything fell apart. He did capture Wilmington but was too late to be of help. Ferguson was killed and his forces were either dead, wounded, or captured. The mountain men had proved their worth again. Riflemen were picking off British soldiers as soon as they showed their heads. The center line of Cornwallis's soldiers heard that there were five thousand Patriots pursuing them. There were only about three hundred Calvary harassing those fleeing, making it seem like there was a lot more men. It was reminiscent of Gideon in the Bible. [8]

After seeing the power of the Kentucky long rifle in action both Joshua and Caleb knew they both wanted one.

The following month, the Articles of Confederation were adopted. This document would now be the basis for how the thirteen colonies would unite and govern themselves as an independent nation.

In Mid-April, Cornwallis army of about twenty-one-hundred men faced Greene's army of about forty-five hundred men Near Greensboro, North Carolina. It was known as the Battle of Guilford Courthouse. Greene used the same tactic he used at Cowpens with three lines. Cornwallis was determined this time and made it to the third line. Greene repulsed the first line of soldiers but realized that he would not be able to continue to do so when the rest of Cornwallis's army reached the third line. He then withdrew. Cornwallis had officially won the battle, but it cost him twenty

---

8. American Revolutionary War, Battle of Cowan's Ford

five percent of his men.

There were other battles in other towns like Hobkirk's Hill, Fort Granby, another Siege at Ninety-Six. At Elizabethtown, North Carolina, Patriot forces were able to fool the loyalist into thinking they had a much larger army against them by calling out fake commands to a phantom army meant to be overheard by the loyalist army. The loyalist leaders were killed, and the loyalist soldiers fled into a ravine which later became known as Tory Hole. [9]

Cornwallis had been stopped. His forces were so depleted that he was forced to return to Virginia to rest and recoup. It was now Washington's opportunity.

---

9. Wikipedia, Battle of Elizabethtown.

Chapter 15

Victory

Washington had requested help from the French, and they sent a fleet up from the Caribbean. Once Washington knew the fleet was coming, he began moving his army from New York to Virginia to rendezvous with General Marquis de Lafayette. The British spotted the French fleet of thirty-seven ships and sent Admiral Hood with fourteen warships to intercept. He did not meet the French fleet until he reached Chesapeake Bay which now had grown to forty-five ships; the other eight had joined after resupplying Lafayette's forces. The naval battle began and lasted three days. In the end, The British fleet suffered more damage and casualties and was forced to withdraw to New York. The battle left the French in control of the Chesapeake area which cut off aid to Cornwallis's army by sea. The battle was known as the Battle of Capes, Chesapeake Bay. [1]

The British had started this whole thing by trying to exhort the colonists for funds to pay for the French and Indian War through a series of acts that infuriated the Americans. Now after slugging it out with the rebels for six

---

1. American Battlefield Trust, Revolutionary War, The Battle of the Capes.

years, they were in even worst shape. There was a lot less enthusiasm for the war in Great Britain. They had run up an even higher debt. Supplies were low, men were exhausted, and the casualties had mounted. Support was dwindling from the loyalists. It was the same on the American side. The difference, however, was that the American Patriots were fighting for their homes and their freedom.

Washington decided to make a bold move. He decided to march his army further south to Yorktown, Virginia. It was there that Cornwallis was recuperating with about nine thousand troops. There were about eight thousand American and French troops moving south. In addition, they were joined by almost twelve thousand militia, American and French soldiers. The French fleet was now in control of the mouth of Chesapeake Bay preventing British ships from coming to help Cornwallis. Cornwallis had put up fortifications to protect his army. Washington's army dug trenches around the fortifications. Washington did not plan to try to scale the fortifications. Instead, he chose to bombard the British troops into submission. The siege began on September 28, 1781. On October 14, the Americans and French forces were able to capture some of the fortifications. October 17, the British sent an officer with a white handkerchief to discuss the terms of surrender. On October 19, Cornwallis surrendered, ending the last major battle of the Revolutionary war. It was ironic that what Cornwallis had planned for Washington is exactly what Washington did to him and in the very same state of Virginia!

There was another lesser battle just before Yorktown, The Battle of Eutaw Springs, South Carolina. It was a battle between the Americans led by Greene versus the British led by Stewart. Green initially drove the British back but then they made a stand at a brick mansion. That stand allowed another British force to join them and the fighting became very heavy. [2]

Joshua and Caleb found themselves in the middle of that fight. They did well initially but when the second force came upon them, musket balls seemed to be flying everywhere. Caleb saw Joshua go down. He had been hit in the left shoulder. A second musket ball hit him in the leg. Caleb ran immediately to his friend who was bleeding profusely out of his wounds. It did not look good. He was unconscious. Caleb shouted for some help. Benjamin came over to see what had happened.

Caleb with tears in his eyes, "Its Joshua, he has been hit. We need to get him out of here." Benjamin called for some more help.

Benjamin took charge, "You grab his legs; I'll grab his arms. We will carry him out."

As they carried him out, Benjamin shouted to the others that came up to cover them while they carried Joshua out of the battlefield. Several of them found British targets coming near and fired on them. The Targets went down and that gave Benjamin and Caleb the opportunity they needed. They got him to the rear of their forces. They found a doctor to check him out. He quickly determined that the musket balls had gone completely through him. That part was good, but he was still bleeding. He told them to put pressure on the wounds front and back to try to stop the bleeding. He said that is all we can do for now; he had to check on some other wounded men and then he would be back. When returned, he saw that Joshua was still bleeding so he asked Caleb for a little black powder. He put it in the shoulder wound and then fired it. There was a bang and a puff of smoke. Joshua yelled. He did the same thing to the leg wound. Then he grabbed some bandages and wrapped them tightly around both wounds.

---

2. American Battlefield Trust, Revolutionary War, Eutaw Springs

He felt for Joshua's pulse it was week but regular.

Doctor explained. "Boys I have done all I can. Only time will tell. You might want to pray for him."

They did. A short time later, Greene pulled all the men back and withdrew. They made a stretcher for Joshua and carried him out. That night Joshua temperature went up a little too high. Caleb kept putting water on his forehead to try to bring it down. It stayed up for two days. It did not look good. On the third day the fever broke. He awoke weak and hungry.

Doctor upon checking Joshua, "I think we got him back, but it is going to be a long hard recovery. The wounds will heal if we do not get them infected, but it will take a lot of exercise, painful exercise, for him to recover the use of that shoulder. The leg should come back quicker."

An officer came by to check on things.

Officer asked pointing to Joshua, "Do you know this man?"

Caleb answered, "Yes, sir. He is my friend. We come from the same place, farms outside of Boston."

Officer added, "You boys are a long way from home. He isn't going to be any more use to us as a soldier. I think the best thing for him is to see if we can get him home when he is able to travel. What is your name soldier?"

"Caleb, sir."

Officer continued, "Well Caleb, since you know him, would you take responsibility for getting him home if I can find a way to get him there?"

Caleb responded, "Yes, sir."

"Good. Let me see what I can do."

The officer left. He came back three days later.

Officer explained. "We have gotten word that Washington is planning something near Yorktown. You are in luck. We are going to move out to meet him so you can go part of the way with us."

A week later, they got word that the French had beaten the British at

Chesapeake Bay.

"God must be favoring you boys." The officer injected, "The French control Chesapeake Bay and we should be able get the two of you on a ship and transport you to Boston that way."

Joshua was feeling better, but his leg hurt, and his shoulder hurt even more. He was happy, however, to hear the news. It took almost three weeks to make the trip to Chesapeake Bay. By then, Joshua was walking or more accurately limping. At least he was moving on his own power. His shoulder still hurt and there was limited motion. It might take as much as two months more to restore as much of his original movement as possible. When they reached Chesapeake Bay, they really did feel that God was watching out for them; they saw a familiar ship at the dock. It was the Rachel! They could not believe it. The soldiers who brought them to the harbor were under orders to seek passage for them on a ship going to Boston. They saw Joshua and Caleb's expression when the saw the Rachel. They asked:

Soldier asked, "Do you know this ship?"

Joshua answered, "Yes sir! We do. This was the ship that brought us down from Boston so we could join up with the Mountain Boys."

Soldier asked, "Do you think you might secure passage on this ship?"

Caleb spotting Jack on board, "Yes, sir. I already see a friendly face."

Caleb shouted, "Jack!"

Jack turned toward him to see who was calling his name. He recognized the two young men with the soldiers.

Jack startled, "Well I'll be darned, if it isn't Joshua and Caleb. How are you boys?"

He got a partial answer to his question when he saw Joshua limping and his left arm in a sling.

A surprised Jack asked, "What happened Josh?"

Joahua trying to downplay the incident, "Well me and some musket balls got a little too intimate. I am doing better now. How are you doing Jack?"

"I can't complain." Jack responded, "We went to the Caribbean and picked up some supplies. Gave some to your Patriot friends. When we saw the French flags flying here at Chesapeake Bay, we decided to come in and see what was going on. What brings you boys here?"

Caleb answered, "We are looking for passage back to Boston. Joshua is no good to the army any more now and I have been charged with responsibility of getting him home."

Jack glad to help, "Well boys, you are in luck. Your bunks await you. I think we will be happy to take you back. Of course, I will have to clear it with the captain, but I am sure it will be alright. Come on board. I think we plan to sail tomorrow morning."

Joshua and Caleb thanked the soldiers for bringing them. The soldiers were pleased that they did not have to search all over the harbor for passage aboard a ship. They bid goodbye to Joshua and Caleb and the young men asked permission to come aboard. "Granted."

The voyage for the most part was uneventful except for one day. The winds increased and the sea conditions grew to just short of gale force conditions. Jack told Joshua and Caleb to stay below. He also told them:

"There is a rope tied to your bunks. "Jack pointing, "It may get a bit rough for a while. The rope is there to tie you in. The Rachel can handle the seas; she has done it many times in the past. Those of us that sail her know what she can do. If you have never been through a storm, it can get rough. Exciting enough so that you could be tossed out of your bunks if you are not tied in."

Joshua and Caleb turned a little pale at that last comment.

Jack grinning, "Don't worry boys; The Rachel knows how to slap the sea down if it gets a little uppity."

Caleb caught on first and smiled back. It was a reference to Jessica slapping Joshua. When he saw Caleb smiling, he realized he had just been kidded about the event. He shook his head with a wry smile.

They survived the storm. They were a little shook up, but The Rachel came through just as Jack had said. It would provide a good story to tell later. A week or so later they were docked in Boston. They said goodbye to Jack and the others onboard the Rachel; then made their way home. They reached Caleb's family home first. Everyone was overjoyed to see them. There were hugs from everyone. Sarah could see that Joshua had been hurt. He was still limping a little and he was not using his left arm as much. She gently touched his arm and looked at him with deep concern in her face.

Sarah in a concerned voice, "What happened, Josh?"

Joshua kidded, "Oh, me and a couple of musket balls decided to dance together."

Sarah responded sternly. "Joshua Rutledge! Don't be so cavalier about this."

Joshua in a more appropriate tone, "I got shot, Sarah, here in my left shoulder and in my leg. They are healing. The leg is doing a better than the arm. The doctor told me that it would take time and a lot of painful exercise but, hopefully, I can get back the total use of my arm."

She gave him a hug, a good one. She then took his face in her hands and kissed him. He loved her hug and her gentle touch, but it was the kiss that reminded him that he really did love her.

Caleb asked his dad if he could borrow the wagon to take Joshua the rest of the way home. He immediately said yes. Sarah insisted that she ride along with them. She held onto Joshua as they rode. The Rutledge's were just as excited and happy to see that the boys made it back home. Each member of Joshua's family gave them hugs. Elizabeth could see that her son had been hurt, it was all over her face.

Seeing the concern on his mother's face he responded, "It is alright, Mom. I got shot in the shoulder and in the leg. They are healing and I think everything will be ok. The leg is almost back to normal. I must keep working the shoulder so I can restore full motion."

"How did it happen?" Still concerned.

Joshua explained, "We were at a place called Eutaw Springs, South Carolina in a fight with some British soldiers. Another contingent joined in the fight and that is when I got wounded. Caleb and some other soldiers got me off the field and to a doctor who stopped the bleeding. He said I was lucky; the musket balls went straight through."

Elizabeth hugged her son. She then saw Sarah nearby with the same look of concern. She motioned to her to come over. They both hugged Joshua and then stepped back. Sarah slipped her arm under Joshua's. She gave Elizabeth a look as if to say:

"I am staying right here until I know he is Ok."

She and Elizabeth have always had a special bond. She knew what Sarah was thinking without her having to say a word. She nodded to Sarah as if to say she understood. Sarah returned the nod.

Chapter 16

The Articles

The Articles of Confederation had been written in 1777 but were not ratified by the states until March of 1781. By the time Joshua and Caleb made it back home, there were copies printed up and distributed so that the colonists could see what the Continental Congress had established as their new government. State constitutions had been in existence for many years, and it was only natural that Congress drew from the wisdom of those documents to create a new one.

The Rutledge's and the Reed's decided to obtain a copy and as they had done with other documents, sit down read and discuss it. Thomas was able to obtain a copy from the tavern in Boston. It did not appear too lengthy, so they decided to do it after church the following Sunday at the Rutledge home. Joshua or Caleb had been the readers in the past but now Mark, Joshua's younger brother asked if he could do it this time instead. They all thought it was a good idea. Mark quickly scanned the first paragraph and realized that it was just an introduction identifying the congress, the states and the date. He told them that he did not think he had to read aloud every state. They all agreed.

Mark explained, "I see the date it was written was the 15th day of November 1777, but it did not get adopted until March of this year, 1781. I wonder why it took so long."

Joshua added, "I am sure the war had something to do with that. It would be dangerous for couriers to try to distribute copies to each state in the middle of this war."

Charles (Caleb's brother) interjected, "I agree."

Both Charles and Caleb's other brother William had also served in the army. It was nowhere near as long as Johua and Caleb, but they knew something of the dangers. The rest encouraged Mark to continue.

Mark read aloud, **"Article I. The Stile of this confederacy shall be, The United States of America."**

Hannah thoughtfully, "That is interesting. They did not give the nation a name like France or Germany. They called it The United States of America."

Mark explained," I think the next article explains why. It says:

'Article II. Each state retains its sovereignty, freedom and independence, and every power, Jurisdiction and right which is not by this confederation expressly delegated to the United States, in Congress assembled.'"

Sarah satisfied, "I think I get it. They wanted a balance between the power of the confederacy and the states. That is smart. The Bible clearly says we are all sinners and prone to do wrong. Too much power in either a single person (a king) or a group of people will likely lead to tyranny and isn't that what this war has been all about, fighting against tyranny?

They all agreed. Thomas, Elizabeth, John and Mary all looked at each other and smiled. They had raised their children to think critically and not just accept blindly what others said. They did not want their children to be like proverbial rats following a pied piper to their destruction. They had seen the results of uncontrolled emotion taking control causing riots, destruction, and even harm to others. They like apparently the Confederacy leaders wanted reason not emotion to ultimately prevail. They were now seeing the fruits of their labor. They were proud of their children.

Caleb commented, "It appears they wanted limited government, only what is necessary to accomplish the goals set for the confederacy."

Mark continued, "The next article seems to lay out some of the goals.

'Article III The said states hereby severally enter into a firm league of friendship with each other, for their common defense, the security of their liberties, and their mutual and general welfare, binding themselves to assist each other, against all force offered to, or attacks made upon them, or any of them, on account of religion, sovereignty, trade, or any other pretense whatever.'"

Joshua: "I think that is clear. You all agree?"

They did.

The next article, Article IV, was longer, so Mark read through it. It laid out the rights of the "free inhabitants" in the states regarding other states. Paupers, vagabonds, and fugitives were not considered free inhabitants.

William in a puzzled tone, "I am not sure that excluding paupers is fair."

"I see your point, William." Sarah interjected but then added, "You think paupers means poor people. A good poor person will seek out work to meet their needs. Historically, however, a pauper is poor and lives off handouts. The Bible indicates that 'If a man will not work, he should not eat.'[1] I think that paupers are more likely to steal to meet their needs rather than work."

Mark continued, "The rest of that paragraph seems to be saying that a citizen of one state should be able to enter and exit another state and enjoy all the privileges of the other state the same as the citizens of that state but also must abide by the laws and restrictions of that state. Did I summarize

---

1. II Thessalonians 3:10

it ok?"

They all agreed that he did.

"The last part of that paragraph seems to be about any restrictions on property removal from state to state. I am not sure I understand that one." Mark conceded.

Caleb responded, "It may have to do with rules on property that are different in one state than another. I may be wrong but suppose one state taxes a piece of property and another state does not. An owner may try to remove the property from the taxing state to the one that does not tax to avoid the tax. Of course, we cannot move land from state to state but maybe something like a saleable commodity, tobacco, cotton, etc. The taxing state would object to moving such property."

The others thought that sounded like a reasonable explanation. For now, they were satisfied and willing to go on.

Mark continued, "the next paragraph addresses criminals that try to escape to another state. The state having jurisdiction has the right to retrieve that criminal." They agreed.

"The last paragraph of that article," Mark added, "indicates that records are to be shared from state to state."

Mark then read through the next article, Article V, and then asked what they thought.

Sarah responded, "The first part of that article seems to be addressing conflicts of interest where a delegate also holds another office."

Joshua agreed, "I think you are right, Sarah. That would be bad. I also like the idea of restricting the time they can serve. I think that might make it more difficult for someone to grab power. Maybe that should be considered for any elective office." Sarah smiled at Joshua.

Mark insisted, "I want to read the last paragraph again; I think it is important.

'Freedom of speech and debate in Congress shall not be impeached or questioned in any court, or place out of Congress, and the members of congress shall be protected in their persons from arrests and imprisonments, during the time of their going to and from and attendance on congress, except for treason, felony, or breach of peace.'"

Thomas emphatically stated, "That should be extended to all of us, period!"

They all said, "Amen!"

Mark continued, "Article VI is long. The first part seems to be saying that the United States government should be the one dealing with any foreign powers and not the individual states. That is one of those rights delegated to Congress. Then it goes on to say that maintaining armies or navies should also be the responsibility of Congress except when the state needs them for defense. The third paragraph also gives Congress the exclusive right to declare and engage in war. They are trying to make it clear those things that are the exclusive right of Congress versus the rights of individual states."

Elizabeth beaming, "Mark, I am so proud of you; I think you nailed it!" They all agreed.

Several articles defined the rights of Congress versus the states. For example, Article VII gave the power to raise land forces to Congress. Article VIII had to do with charges incurred in war. The monies were to come out of the common treasury but filling that treasury was the responsibility and control of the individual states. Article IX gives Congress the right to make decisions in war and peace. Congress was also to be the last resort when disputes arose between the states. Congress was also to have the exclusive right to print money and fix standards of weights and measures.

The rest of the Articles were read quickly without a lot of discussion, but one point mentioned in Articles IX and X, raised a little concern with Thomas and John after they thought about it.

Thomas questioning, "If I understand this correctly, nine states are required to make certain decisions."

Elizabeth puzzled, "So what are you concerned about, that would be a majority of states?"

Thomas explained, "What concerns me is that if five states banded together and disagreed with something, they could prevent that thing happening even though the majority of the states voted for the thing."

Joshua interjected, "I get it, five states would have veto power over the other eight states. I think you are right, Dad, I am not sure that is going to work."

Thomas thoughtfully, "Well time will tell. Right now, that is what we have."

About this time, they were all getting hungry, so they brought out some food. They talked with each other for a while and then the Reed's went on home except for Sarah. She said she would come back before dark but would help Elizabeth clean up. That was just an excuse to spend time with Joshua. Elizabeth and Mary had already pretty much cleaned up everything. Neither family was fooled; they knew that Sarah was sweet on Joshua.

Chapter 17

Reunion

The Rachel continued to Halifax after leaving Joshua and Caleb in Boston. There she would unload some cargo and take on more before she left in a few days. As sailors will often do in port, they searched a favorite tavern for some relaxation and a brew or two. As Jack was approaching the tavern, a familiar face happened to walk by him. It was the girl that had slapped Joshua the first time he had brought Joshua and Caleb to Halifax. He was surprised to see her. Jessica saw his face and knew that he looked familiar. She stopped for a moment and said:

"I think I know you."

Jack explained, "Yes you do. It has been a while, but you are hard to forget. You walked up boldly to our ship in the harbor to a passenger of ours, kissed him, and then promptly slapped him on the face. I ain't likely to forget that." Jessica's eyes widened.

"You brought Joshua and Caleb here!"

Jack added, "Yes little lady, we did. Brought him back to Boston too, a few days ago."

A surprised Jessica responded, "He is in Boston?"

Jack: "Yes, my name is Jack. I am not sure I remember your name although I will never forget you."

"I am Jessica. Is Joshua, ok?"

"He will be." Jack attempted to calm her. "He was wounded in some battle somewhere in the south, twice actually. He took a musket ball in the shoulder and another one in his leg. Caleb was bringing him back home."

Jessica alarmed, "Oh my God! Is he alright? I must go to him."

Jack trying to change the tone, "You want to go and slap him again for getting shot?"

Jessica in a different voice, "No, no, of course not. I just care about him."

Jack could see his joke was not being received and that he was dealing with a very concerned young woman that really did care about Joshua.

Jack insisted, "Calm down, he is alright. He is healing. He is walking some on the leg. His shoulder is healing as well but it will take longer. He is probably out of the war now."

Jessica took a deep breath and calmed herself. Her mind began to think about what she wanted to do. She wanted to go to Joshua but how to get there was a problem.

Jessica collecting her thoughts asked, "Is your ship going back to Boston anytime soon?"

Jack responded, "Yes, in three days. We tend to make regular stops between Halifax, Boston and the Caribbean."

With that answer she worked out her plan.

"Will you take me to Boston?" Jessica asked.

Jack a bit hesitant, "Well, I do not know about that. We have never taken a woman on board before."

Jessica would not be put off, "You have taken passengers before; you took Joshua and Caleb."

Jack answered, "Yes, but that was different."

Jessica indignantly, "How so? A passenger is a passenger."

Jack a little flustered, "I know but we aren't equipped to handle a woman passenger."

Jessica was adamant, "Do you think a British warship is more equipped, because that is how I came here from Boston in the first place?"

Jack completely flustered, "Well no, but…"

Jessica added, "I can pay you and there will be no need for special treatment other than a little privacy at times."

Jack realizing he was not going to win an argument with this young lady.

"I will have to bring this up with the captain."

Jack insisted, "Good. I assume you were heading to the tavern over there." she pointed to the tavern called

'The Harp and Crown'."

Jack said, "yes."

Jessica pointing beyond the tavern, "Down the street a little way is my father's dry goods store called 'Pitman's Dry Goods". You will find me there."

Jack asked, "How will you make your way around Boston?"

Jessica in a softer tone, "Thank you for your concern but that is not a problem. Boston was my home, and my aunt and uncle still live there. I will have no problem there. Will you take my request to your captain?"

Jack responded, "Yes. I will get back to you tomorrow about this same time (it was about 5PM).

We would not sail until the next day."

Jack left Jessica and headed to the tavern. He may need more than two brews now.

Jessica finished what she had intended to do before she met Jack and then headed back to the store. She mulled over how she was going to approach her father. That was going to be a big hurdle. She did not think she could tell him the real reason she wanted to go to Boston; her father was never in favor of her relationship with Joshua. She could hear him now in her mind telling her that she should set her sights higher, someone in her class like another merchant. She had those discussions in the past. They always ended in her being estranged from her father for a while. She would have to think of another reason for going to Boston; something that he might accept, even think it was a good thing.

She pondered it for a while and then she worked out the perfect solution. She would ask her father if she could visit her aunt and uncle. Her aunt had practically raised her after her mother died. She would tell him that she missed her, which was true, that it had been a long time since she had seen either of them. She could also use his desire for her to become more acquainted with the business. She worked all the details out in her head. She was good at that and knew it. She also knew her father and how to persuade him. It would take a little more planning to "find a ship going to Boston and discover the Rachel". She would also have to make sure that Jack and the other sailors did not spoil her plan by letting on her true motive for the trip.

The next day, Jack told her that it would be alright with the captain if it was alright with her father. He also suggested a fare for the trip. Jessica thought the amount was reasonable and she had enough of her own money to pay it. She anticipated that she might have difficulty convincing her father of a trip to Boston if he found out that she had already secured passage. She made Jack swear to secrecy and never let on he knew her. He did.

Jessica thought the best way to get her father to agree to the trip was to try to make it seem as if it was his idea. She would have to work fast; she only had a day to do it. She knew her father, she knew what buttons to push. She had always been his favorite; Jessica thought it was because she reminded him so much of her mother. He had dearly loved her, and it was a terrible time for him when she died in childbirth. She formed her plan and began to execute it that evening. She talked to him how much she missed Boston, her aunt, and her uncle. She also teared up a little as she told him. Jessica really did miss them, especially her aunt Martha. She was very young when her mother died and barely remembered her. Aunt Martha stepped in and assumed the mother role. The tears were more to persuade her father. She waited a little while.

Jessica sighing, "I wish we could go see them."

She waited a bit more and allowed a few more tears to trickle down her face. She knew her father hated to see her sad.

Jessica with more emphasis, "I miss Boston too and some of my friends that may still be there."

She sighed for effect. She could see she had his attention, now she needed to let the thought of visiting Boston simmer a bit. She left him for a while and later came back with a sad forlorn look on her face. She needed to convince her father that only a visit to Boston would make her happy.

Father concerned for his daughter, "Are you still sad?"

Jessica in a sad tone, "Oh, I will be alright, I just miss Aunt Martha so much (another tear came down her face)."

Father relented a little, "Well, maybe we can plan a trip next year sometime."

She knew she had succeeded in planting the suggestion of a trip. Now she needed to move up the timeline. She brightened up when her father said that and then made her face sad again.

Jessica with an even sadder tone, "Do we have to wait that long, that seems like forever?"

She came over and kissed her father, a gesture of submission, but sighed as she did it. She now needed to wait a bit to let it take effect. Her father absolutely hated to see those sad eyes. Jessica knew exactly what she was doing.

It took a little more time, but she finally got her father to say that he would investigate any ships going to Boston. She immediately brightened and then asked:

Jessica brightened, "Can I go to the docks with you; I love to see the ships?"

He agreed. He was happy to see her brighten up. She knew about where the Rachel was docked so she was able to maneuver him to that location. When they came close, she saw Jack on deck. She gave him a look to remind him that he did not know her. Jack saw it and nodded slightly.

Jack feigning not knowing Jessica, "Hello there, can I be of help?"

Father responded, "Yes, let me introduce myself. I am John Pitman. I was wondering if this ship will be headed to Boston anytime soon and if so, if we can secure passage aboard her?"

Jack held out his hand, "Glad to meet you Mr. Pitman. Just call me Jack. As a matter of fact, we are, day after tomorrow. I will have to confer with the captain about passage, but I am sure it will be alright. We have done it before (he smiled very slightly while looking at Jessica). Will that be for just you sir or the young lady as well?"

John responded, "It would be for the both of us."

Jack asked, "Ok, where can I contact you?"

John answered, "We have a store near the end of the dock called Pitman's Dry Goods."

Jessica added, "It is near the Harp and Crown Tavern with which you may be familiar."

Jack responded, "Yes, I am. Your store should not be hard to find."

John a little concerned, "Jessica, how do you know about the Harp and Crown Tavern?"

Jessica chastising her father a little, "Father, I walk the docks all the time, you can't miss it near our store."

John more concerned, "You have not been there, have you?"

Jessica indignantly, "Of course not! How could you ask such a thing?"

Her mild scolding convinced her father that it was nothing.

She had not objected to her father making the trip with her. It was only proper. Ladies just did not travel by themselves, especially on a ship with people they would not know. Besides, a father is supposed to protect his child. She also knew that the business concerns here in Halifax would eventually concern her father so he would not wish to be gone too long. Jessica would just need to convince him to allow her to stay in Boston for an extended length of time. She did not think that would be hard. Aunt Martha after all was like a mother to her. Her aunt and uncle had always been happy to see her. She laid out a plan in her mind and then thought about Joshua. She put on a bright happy face, partly for her father but also because she was indeed happy about her plan had succeeded. When they returned to the store, she made sure that her father got a big hug and every other reward that she could think of.

***

The trip to Boston was relatively uneventful. Jack was true to his word and did not reveal that he knew Jessica prior to his meeting with her father.

When she was alone on the ship, she thought about Joshua. She remembered their lunches together on the side of the store. She recalled his shyness and how she had to probe a bit to get him to talk to her. She could read him; she knew when he was upset, when he was happy, when he did not like something said. He could not hide it from her. He talked a lot about his family, the farm, and Caleb. He seemed excited about life, watching new life coming into the world, things growing. They had some pretty energized discussions about the British acts against the Colonists. She also knew that he hated having her upset with him. He would back off and keep his thoughts to himself when that happened. She did not like that so much; she liked a good scrap every now and then. She loved those beautiful eyes, looking at her as though she was the most beautiful person in the entire world. It was captivating. She wanted that look all the time.

Her thoughts eventually came to Sarah. She did not know her. She tried to picture her as some kind of evil witch that she could get angry at for "stealing" her Joshua. How dare she do that. Surely Joshua would not have fallen for a witch. She wondered what she looked like. What was her personality? What did he see in her that allured him? He told her that they had grown up together. He had known her all his life. These thoughts invaded her mind. She would have to suppress them around her father. She had to maintain a happy countenance about the trip to Boston. She did not want him to discover the real reason for the trip.

It took a day or two longer to return from Halifax to Boston than the reverse trip. Going south, the ship had to fight the northward current prevalent along the coast. The winds were fair, and they safely made the trip.

Her aunt and uncle were surprised but happy to see them both. They had missed them as well; especially Aunt Martha. Jessica had been her daughter even if she had not physically given her birth. They greeted each other, hugged each other, and talked for quite a while about things in Boston, things in Halifax and how everyone was doing.

Martha asked, "How long are you planning to stay?"

"I do not think we can stay too long." John explained. "We must get back to Halifax, the business you know."

Jessica was now about to execute the next phase of her plan:

Jessica in a calm voice, "Dad, you need to get back but there is no pressing reason why I have to."

John thought about it, "Well that is true, but we do not want to impose, Jessica."

Jessica knew her aunt would step in, and she did.

"Oh, come on John, let Jessica stay." Martha insisted. "We always love to see her. She is welcome to stay as long as she likes. Besides, that will be one less worry on your mind and you can concentrate on the business."

Jessica smiled slightly. She knew her father well enough that he would not stand up to two women with one mindset. He gave in and agreed to let Jessica stay. The next day, he searched for passage back to Halifax, found as ship leaving in three days and secured passage.

Jessica was dying to go see Joshua but needed to wait until her father left. After he did, she talked with her aunt. Aunt Martha was aware of Joshua and Jessica's feelings for him. Jessica could hide things from her father but not her aunt. She told her that she had gotten word that Joshua was home but had been wounded in battle. She asked her aunt if she knew where the Rutledge farm was. Her aunt did; she had spoken several times with Elizabeth, Joshua's mother, and had even given to Elizabeth Jessica's address in Halifax. Aunt Martha had a surrey at her disposal and the two of them headed out to the Rutledge farm the next day. It was midmorning when they arrived.

Elizabeth saw them coming and when they got closer, she recognized them both.

Elizabeth smiled as they approached, "Hello Martha, and you too Jessica."

Martha responded, "Hello Elizabeth."

Jessica wondered how Elizabeth knew her.

Elizabeth seeing the puzzled look on Jessica's face, "Jessica, you waited on me once in your father's store. Also, I know about you and my son. He cannot hide anything from me; he never could. I assume you have come to see him."

Jessica responded, "Yes, if it is ok."

Elizabeth smiled, "Of course, please come in. Sarah is giving him some therapy on his shoulder right now, but I am sure he will be glad to see you."

Hearing the name, Sarah brought Jessica a moment of reflection. She had not counted on meeting her so soon. She took a deep breath, got down off the surrey and went in. Elizabeth motioned them toward the back bedroom where Sarah was working Joshua's arm. Martha stayed out with Elizabeth while Jessica went in. Joshua did not see her right away; Sarah was lifting his arm as high as it would go. It was a painful maneuver, and the pain showed on his face."

Jessica concern in her voice, "What are you doing to him?"

Joshua heard her voice and looked up at her shocked.

Sarah explained, "I know it looks bad, but this is the only way that Joshua will ever recover the total use of his arm."

"She is right;" Joshua agreed. "I have asked her to do this for me. We must do these fifty or more times a day to stretch the ligaments and muscles. I am gradually getting the use of my arm back."

Jessica for once did not know what to say. It was Sarah who came to her rescue.

Sarah held out her hand to Jessica, "I am Sarah Caleb's sister. You must be Jessica."

Jessica took her hand, "Yes"

Sarah turned toward Joshua, "Josh, we can do this later; I am sure you want to talk to Jessica." Sarah then faced Jessica, "I will leave the two of you alone, I am glad to meet you, Jessica."

Jessica nodded. She expected her womanly senses to all be on fire meeting Sarah, but they weren't. Sarah's voice was gentle, kind, and even soothing.

She saw her put her hand on Joshua's arm. It was a gentle loving touch. He smiled slightly but then Jessica could see the conflict rising in his eyes. Sarah then left and closed the door.

Jessica came over to Joshua and gave him a long and tender hug. Then she pulled away.

"I should slap you again;" Jessica scolded,

"you went off and almost got yourself killed!"

Joshua insisted, "I did not plan this, Jessica."

"I know." She said in a calmer voice, "I just hate seeing you hurt. I am glad that you are home, though."

Joshua agreed, "Me too."

Jessica asked, "Is Caleb alright?"

Joshua responded, "Yes, he was unhurt but helped me get home. He is home too."

Jessica asked, "Does this mean you are out of the war?"

"Yes," responded Joshua, "and I believe the war is coming to an end, although it may take a while before everyone everywhere knows it."

Jessica in a softer tone, "I missed you, Joshua."

Joshua did not respond right away, which pained her.

"You know I love you." She responded,

Joshua answered, "Yes and I love you too."

Jessica in concerned voice, "What are we going to do?"

"I do not know." responded Joshua.

The conflict in his eyes was intense. She touched his arm as Sarah had done. He responded by putting his hand gently on hers. She knew then that he still loved her but also that he loved Sarah. That was his conflict, and he did not know how to resolve it. He loved both and absolutely hated hurting either of them. It was tearing him apart. She hugged him again, and after a little time, went out to let him rest.

Jessica asked Elizabeth if it would be alright if she came and helped with Joshua's therapy. Elizabeth wished she wouldn't, but also knew that Joshua, Sarah, and Jessica would have to resolve the conflict without her interference. She told Jessica it would be ok. Over the next couple of weeks, she came every day. Sarah showed her what to do to lift his arm as high as it would go, hold it and then bring it back down. Each time it would hurt him, but that was the only way to stretch the ligaments and muscles to gain back full motion. It was pain with a purpose. Sarah hated hurting Joshua. She was a little conflicted because in one sense she wanted to be the only one attending Joshua and yet she was glad to be relieved. It wasn't long before Jessica began to feel the same way. They performed the exercises five or six times each day, each time raising the arm ten to twelve times.

Jessica watched Sarah, her family, Joshua's family, and their interactions with each other. When she came, she was seeking information to help her plan how she would win Joshua away from Sarah. She had thought about it even as she was sailing to Boston on the Rachel. As she interacted more and more with everyone, especially Sarah, she felt bad about her attitude. Sarah was genuinely nice to her. Her senses told her there was no ulterior motive. She could see that Sarah was deeply in love with Joshua. His interaction with Sarah confirmed what he had openly confessed to her, that he was in love with Sarah. Yet Jessica also had felt and seen Joshua's love.

Jessica also watched the interaction with the rest of Joshua's family. There was warmth, respect, and love there. This family was living out the image portrayed in the Bible of what a family should be. Like the Rutledge's and the Reed's, she had grown up with the Bible and church. She had attended a Presbyterian church and knew the Bible stories. Her aunt had talked with her often about such things. When she was younger, her aunt had told her about Jesus and showed her from the Bible how he had died for her sins. Her aunt had led her in a prayer to put her trust in

Jesus.

Being with these two families was now teaching her some living Bible lessons acted before her eyes. One day Jessica observed Thomas watching Elizabeth from a little distance away without her knowing. His look was precious, loving, gentle, kind, and proud. This was his mate. Jessica saw before her eyes a living portrayal of the Bible idea of marriage that "they shall be one flesh."[1] Later, she observed John and Mary Reed interacting with each other. She saw the same look in John's eyes when he looked at Mary. It was an indescribable look but one that every woman would want from her man. When she looked close at Elizabeth and Mary, she also saw the same look from them toward their husbands. They were connected in a way that only God could do.

She also observed Sarah with Joshua. She stood beside him, helping him, but did not try to rule him. She remembered the Bible verses that said that a woman was to submit to her husband. At the time she thought that was old-fashioned and not for this modern world. As she recalled those verses, she remembered again what her aunt had said to her many years ago. The same thing that came to mind when she first met Joshua.

"A woman is never powerful than when she stands as a helpmate beside her man."

Jessica remembered thinking at the time that it was a weird thing to remember. Sarah was submitting to Joshua even if it meant that he would choose against her. Jessica also was a little ashamed of her attitude; she came to manipulate the situation in her favor. She had done it before; she thought of her father. Sarah was being a helpmate, she was planning on how to win the prize, Joshua.

---

1. Genesis 2:24

Each day Jessica would leave to go back into Boston to her aunt and uncle. At first, she rode away in the surrey alone. She realized quickly that Sarah was walking home and, as much as she at first resented her rival, she knew it was not right to let her walk. She offered her a ride, which at first Sarah politely resisted. Jessica insisted and after that took her home every evening. They began to talk along the way. Jessica realized that Sarah knew quite a bit about her; Joshua had spoken often about their lunches together and his feelings. Joshua had grown up with Sarah. She had always been part of his life as far back as he could remember. Sarah told her that Joshua had always looked out for her and protected her.

Jessica asked, "When did you know that you were in love with Joshua?"

Sarah answered, "I think it started all the way back when I was little. I used to dream about him and I sharing a life together."

It dawned on Jessica that Sarah may not have been the other woman. Sarah was genuine and honest and try as she might, Jessica could not detect any guile in her. Soon, Jessica began to pick Sarah up on her way to the Rutledge's as well as take her home. The more time she spent with her, the more she had to admit she liked her.

After two weeks of therapy, it was obvious that Joshua's shoulder was much better. He had almost full motion and strength.

Sarah quietly, "I will not be coming with you anymore. I think Joshua is well healed and does not need me anymore."

Jessica could see that Sarah had been crying although she was trying to hide it.

Sarah continued, "I can see the conflict in his face, and it is killing me. I hate it. I want him to be happy not conflicted. I am causing that conflict, so I am going to stay away. Just take care of him for me." Jessica turned quickly; tears filled her eyes, and she quickly walked away. When she went back to town, her aunt could see that Jessica was distraught.

Martha seeing how sad Jessica appeared, "Are you alright, dear?

Jessica answered, "No."

She then told her aunt what had happened.

Martha responded, "I am not sure I understand. Isn't Sarah your rival for Joshua's affection? She seems to be giving him to you."

Jessica elaborated, "Over these last couple of weeks, I have gotten to know Sarah well. I like her. She loves Joshua as much, maybe more than I do. She just wants to take away the conflict in his mind and is willing to give him up to do it."

Martha responded, "Wow! As you were talking, I remember a Bible story in the Old Testament."

"What story?" she asked.

"It's about two women coming before Solomon each has had a child and one of the children has died. Each woman claims the living child is hers. Solomon is being asked to decide between the two women."

"I remember it, but how does that relate to my situation?" Jessica asked.

Martha continued, "Solomon tells his men to cut the living child in two and give each half to the two women."

Jessica alarmed, "Wow! That is drastic!"

"Yes," Martha continued, "but it did not happen. The real mother told him to give the child to the other woman. She loved her child enough to give him up and let him live. Solomon then knew who the real mother was and gave the child to her. Jessica, it sounds like Sarah loves Joshua enough to give him up and resolve the conflict, just like the real mother in the Bible."[2]

"Aunt Martha, you always seem to know me. You have been a mother

---

2. I Kings 3:16-28

to me; you always give me good advice. What do you think I should do?" Jessica asked.

Martha answered, "I am not sure, but I think you should ask yourself whether Joshua would be happier with you or Sarah going forward."

Jessica thought about what her aunt told her. Joshua was a farmer. The things that seemed to excite him were all about life, the land, the wonder of nature. He never seemed to be that interested in the mercantile business or society. It dawned on Jessica that if she were to win over Sarah, she would be dragging him into a life that may not make him happy. It would make her happy, but not him. That thought pained her. For the first time she was thinking more about him and not about herself. Tears flooded her eyes.

For the next week, she visited Joshua alone. The first day, he asked about Sarah. She told him that Sarah had decided that she had done all she could do and did not need to be there. Each day, Joshua would greet her as he always did, but she could tell he was missing Sarah; he never could keep things from her. When the week was done, she now knew what she needed to do, but she absolutely did not want to do it. Another Bible passage came to mind about Jesus. It was in the Garden of Gethsemane where he was stressed about having to go to the cross.

"O my father, if it be possible, let this cup pass from me: nevertheless, not as I will, but as thou wilt."[3]

She needed to take away Joshua's conflict and free him. She quickly prayed that if there was any other way... She realized there was no other way. Sarah had known it too. Jesus saw that with mankind and needed to take the burden of sin on himself so that mankind could be free. He did it out of love.

---

3. Matthew 26:39

"For God so loved the world that he gave his only begotten son that whoso-ever believeth in him should not perish but have everlasting life."[4]

If she really loved Joshua, she must take away his pain. She would have to take it on herself and give him his freedom. Tears flooded her eyes as she thought about how to do it.

The next day, she went to the Reed house and told Sarah to come with her. Sarah resisted, but Jessica insisted; she had something she wanted to say to both her and Joshua together. When they arrived at the Rutledge house, Joshua greeted her as usual and was pleasantly surprised to see Sarah and greeted her as well. It was pleasant enough outside, so they sat together on the porch.

Jessica in a measured voice, "I have something I want to say to the both of you. I have thought about things while I have been here. I can see Joshua, and how much your family, this place, and your life here means to you. I have seen the love you all share. I also have come to realize that you would not be happy living in town or in Halifax. It just is not you. While I have enjoyed the hospitality all of you have extended to me, I also know that I would probably not make a good farmer's wife. Joshua, you need a mate that shares your dreams and aspirations. I am not sure that I can be that for you."

At that point she was doing her best to hold back the tears. She took Joshua's hand and Sarah's hand. Joshua could not see the pain behind her words and actions, but Sarah could.

Jessica continued, "You have someone, Joshua, that already shares those aspirations and dreams."

As she said it, she placed Sarah's hand in his and then placed both her

---

4. John 3:16

hands over both their hands.

Jessica looking into his eyes, "Joshua, I will always love you; I will always have fond memories of you."

She then looked at Sarah.

"Sarah, I have come to know you these past weeks. I now believe that you are God's chosen mate for Joshua."

Jessica was about at the end of her strength and needed to exit. She got up at that point, moved toward the porch steps. Elizabeth came out and could see immediately that something had transpired. Jessica said her goodbyes to Elizabeth and began walking toward her surrey. Sarah followed her.

Sarah softly called her, "Jessica."

Jessica did not turn around; her eyes were flooded now with tears. Sarah came around in front of her, saw her face, and hugged her.

Sarah whispering, "Thank you"

Jessica responded, "Please take care of him."

Sarah said as she held her, "I will."

Elizabeth sensed what had happened. She came out, saw the tears, and gave Jessica a hug also. Sarah saw Joshua coming out and warned Jessica. Jessica took out a handkerchief and quickly wiped her eyes. She took a deep breath and composed herself. When she saw Joshua's face, she knew she had done the right thing; the pain and conflict were gone. She just needed to hold out a little longer. He came up to her and she hugged him. She then put one hand on his face and kissed his cheek. There was a different look on his face, the conflict was replaced by concern. She knew him; it warmed her a bit that he was concerned for her.

Jessica putting on her best calm in control voice, "Don't worry about me, Joshua, there have been a number of suitors and protectors."

"Protector, like the one in Halifax?" Joshua asked,

"Yes, his name is Brian; he has been trying for a long time to court me."

Jessica could see the concern on Joshua's face ease a bit. She had convinced him that she would be alright.

She then got into her surrey and rode off. She would grieve for a while, but it would pass. She had not lied to Joshua about other suitors in her life, even the "protector" at the Halifax store. He had been trying to court her for some time now. Maybe in a while she would let him. When she was a little way off, she looked back. Joshua was free. Maybe she was too. She saw Sarah giving him a long lingering kiss. Jessica thought to herself:

"She is getting a taste of freedom."

Chapter 18

Aftermath

Even though Yorktown was the last major battle of the war, it would take time to officially end the war. It took at least six weeks for the news to reach England and more time to process the information. It was March the following year that the British Parliament passed legislation to authorize peace negotiations. It would take another year for Congress to ratify a preliminary peace treaty and five more months for the United States and Great Britain to officially sign it in Paris. [1] Time was a new enemy. That new enemy created more casualties.

The British did not evacuate Savannah until July the following year. There were other smaller raids and skirmishes still going on, like Hannahstown, Pennsylvania also in July, Blue Licks, Kentucky the following month, John's Ferry, South Carolina in November. There were others, especially out on the western frontiers.

It was Ben Franklin among others that was instrumental in negotiating with France and England and securing the final peace treaty. It was signed by the United States and Great Britain on September 3, 1783. [2]

---

1. American Battlefield Trust, Yorktown, Siege of Yorktown

2. American Battlefield Trust, The Treaty Of Paris

Over time, the British evacuated the cities they controlled. Savannah was the first in mid-July 1782. Charleston was next in mid-December. They did not leave New York City until after the Peace Treaty was signed at the end of November 1783.

Approximately two-hundred-thirty-thousand men served in the Continental army but not all at one time. To put this in perspective, the total population of the colonists was about two-point-five million people. If we consider that at least one-point-five million were women and children (the estimate could be higher), then about one million were men. Twenty to twenty-five percent of the men then served in the war. Every family was affected.

Washington never had more than a total of forty-eight-thousand men and never more than thirteen thousand at any one battle. About seven thousand African Americans fought on the Continental side, but what is interesting is that another twenty thousand fought on the British side even knowing that if the British won, their status would not change. France added about twelve thousand in 1779. The British forces numbered about twenty-two thousand men along with about thirty thousand Hessian mercenaries. The British also recruited about twenty-five-thousand loyalists. Native Americans also fought at times, some on either side. There were about sixty-eight-hundred Americans killed, sixty-one hundred wounded, but the biggest toll came from disease: about seventeen thousand. Eight to twelve thousand were prisoners. Some estimated the British losses to be about twenty-four thousand from death, disease, and injuries. The Hessians lost about twelve hundred killed and sixty-three hundred to disease. Interestingly, the Hessians lost another five thousand nine hundred men who disserted and later settled in America. [3]

The war left scars. There was animosity, Americans against the British and Hessians, Americans against other Americans, Americans against the Native American Indians. As many as One hundred thousand loyalists left the colonies to settle in Canada, Nova Scotia, or other British colonies. [4]

Native Americans were another concern. The Colonies needed to heal.

---

3. American Battlefield Trust, American Revolution Facts

4. Wikipedia, Expulsion of the Loyalists

They had fought for freedom against tyranny. Now they would have to see how they would live with the freedom to govern themselves. The Articles of Confederation provided a starting point. Some felt that it may not work because there was too much power given to the states and not enough to the union. Only time would tell. In any case, they needed to work with what they had to lay a solid foundation for freedom.

Appendices

Declaration of Independence In Congress, July 4, 1776

The unanimous Declaration of the thirteen united States of America, When in the Course of human events, it becomes necessary for one people to dissolve the political bands which have connected them with another, and to assume among the powers of the earth, the separate and equal station to which the Laws of Nature and of Nature's God entitle them, a decent respect to the opinions of mankind requires that they should declare the causes which impel them to the separation.

We hold these truths to be self-evident, that all men are created equal, that they are endowed by their Creator with certain unalienable Rights, that among these are Life, Liberty and the pursuit of Happiness.--That to secure these rights, Governments are instituted among Men, deriving their just powers from the consent of the governed, --That whenever any Form of Government becomes destructive of these ends, it is the Right of the People to alter or to abolish it, and to institute new Government, laying its foundation on such principles and organizing its powers in such form, as to them shall seem most likely to effect their Safety and Happiness. Prudence, indeed, will dictate that Governments long established should not be changed for light and transient causes; and accordingly all experience hath shewn, that mankind are more disposed to suffer, while evils are sufferable, than to right themselves by abolishing the forms to which they are accustomed. But when a long train of abuses and usurpations, pursuing invariably the same Object evinces a design to reduce them under absolute Despotism, it is their right, it is their duty, to throw off such Government, and to provide new Guards for their future security.--Such has been the patient sufferance of these Colonies; and such is now the necessity which constrains them to alter their former Systems of Government. The history of the present King of Great Britain is a history of repeated injuries and usurpations, all having in direct object the establishment of an absolute Tyranny over these States. To prove this, let Facts be submitted to a candid world.

He has refused his Assent to Laws, the most wholesome and necessary for the public good.

He has forbidden his Governors to pass Laws of immediate and pressing importance, unless suspended in their operation till his Assent should be obtained; and when so suspended, he has utterly neglected to attend to them.

He has refused to pass other Laws for the accommodation of large districts of people, unless those people would relinquish the right of Representation in the Legislature, a right inestimable to them and formidable to tyrants only.

He has called together legislative bodies at places unusual, uncomfortable, and distant from the depository of their public Records, for the sole purpose of fatiguing them into compliance with his measures.

He has dissolved Representative Houses repeatedly, for opposing with manly firmness his invasions on the rights of the people.

He has refused for a long time, after such dissolutions, to cause others to be elected; whereby the Legislative powers, incapable of Annihilation, have returned to the People at large for their exercise; the State remaining in the mean time exposed to all the dangers of invasion from without, and convulsions within.

He has endeavoured to prevent the population of these

States; for that purpose obstructing the Laws for Naturalization of Foreigners; refusing to pass others to encourage their migrations hither, and raising the conditions of new Appropriations of Lands.

He has obstructed the Administration of Justice, by refusing his Assent to Laws for establishing Judiciary powers.

He has made Judges dependent on his Will alone, for the tenure of their offices, and the amount and payment of their salaries.

He has erected a multitude of New Offices, and sent hither swarms of Officers to harrass our people, and eat out their substance.

He has kept among us, in times of peace, Standing Armies without the Consent of our legislatures.

He has affected to render the Military independent of and superior to the Civil power.

He has combined with others to subject us to a jurisdiction foreign to our constitution, and unacknowledged by our laws; giving his Assent to their Acts of pretended Legislation:

For Quartering large bodies of armed troops among us:

For protecting them, by a mock Trial, from punishment for any Murders which they should commit on the Inhabitants of these States:

For cutting off our Trade with all parts of the world:

For imposing Taxes on us without our Consent:

For depriving us in many cases, of the benefits of Trial by Jury:

For transporting us beyond Seas to be tried for pretended offences:

For abolishing the free System of English Laws in a neighbouring Province, establishing therein an Arbitrary government, and enlarging its Boundaries so as to render it at once an example and fit instrument for introducing the same absolute rule into these Colonies:

For taking away our Charters, abolishing our most valuable Laws, and altering fundamentally the Forms of our Governments:

For suspending our own Legislatures, and declaring themselves invested with power to legislate for us in all cases whatsoever.

He has abdicated Government here, by declaring us out of his Protection and waging War against us.

He has plundered our seas, ravaged our Coasts, burnt our towns, and destroyed the lives of our people.

He is at this time transporting large Armies of foreign Mercenaries to compleat the works of death, desolation and tyranny, already begun with circumstances of Cruelty & perfidy scarcely paralleled in the most barbarous ages, and totally unworthy the Head of a civilized nation.

He has constrained our fellow Citizens taken Captive on the high Seas to bear Arms against their Country, to become the executioners of their friends and Brethren, or to fall themselves by their Hands.

He has excited domestic insurrections amongst us, and has endeavoured to bring on the inhabitants of our frontiers, the merciless Indian Savages, whose known rule of warfare, is an undistinguished destruction of all ages, sexes and conditions.

In every stage of these Oppressions We have Petitioned for Redress in the most humble terms: Our repeated Petitions have been answered only by repeated injury. A Prince whose character is thus marked by every act which may define a Tyrant, is unfit to be the ruler of a free people.

Nor have We been wanting in attentions to our Brittish brethren. We have warned them from time to time of attempts by their legislature to extend an unwarrantable jurisdiction over us. We have reminded them of the circumstances of our emigration and settlement here. We have appealed to their native justice and magnanimity, and we have conjured them by the ties of our common kindred to disavow these usurpations, which, would inevitably interrupt our connections and correspondence. They too have been deaf to the voice of justice and of consanguinity. We must, therefore, acquiesce in the necessity, which denounces our Separation, and hold them, as we hold the rest of mankind, Enemies in War, in Peace Friends.

We, therefore, the Representatives of the united States of America, in General Congress, Assembled, appealing to the Supreme Judge of the world for the rectitude of our intentions, do, in the Name, and by Authority of the good People of these Colonies, solemnly publish and declare,

That these United Colonies are, and of Right ought to be Free and Independent States; that they are Absolved from all Allegiance to the British Crown, and that all political connection between them and the State of Great Britain, is and ought to be totally dissolved; and that as Free and Independent States, they have full Power to levy War, conclude Peace, contract Alliances, establish Commerce, and to do all other Acts and Things which Independent States may of right do. And for the support of this Declaration, with a firm reliance on the protection of divine Providence, we mutually pledge

to each other our Lives, our Fortunes and our sacred Honor. [1]

---

1. www.archives/founding-docs/declaration-transscript